"I'll show you a fantasy fling you won't forget."

"Don't." Natalie pressed herself into the door, avoiding Demitri's touch. "Please don't touch me. I have to face people when I leave here, and—"

"You don't want to go back there obviously aroused?" he challenged, needing to hear it—to see it in the helpless flush and the disconcerted casting of her gaze around the room before she brought it back to his, her eyes deeply shadow̲e̲d̲ ̲ ̲ ̲ ̲ ̲ ire.

He presse̲d̲ ̲ ̲ ̲ ̲ ̲ ̲ ̲ ̲ ̲ side her head, leani̲ ̲ ̲ ̲ ̲ ̲ ̲ ̲ ̲ warm peach scen̲ ̲ ̲ ̲ ̲ ̲ ̲ ̲ ̲ raze of her rising b̲ ̲ ̲ ̲ ̲ ̲ ̲ ̲ below his belt, a heavy ̲ ̲ ̲ ̲ of blood pulled him tight.

Flustered and anxious, she still managed to send a coy glance south. Her body arched ever so slightly and she brushed against him. She released a powerless whimper on a sobbing, "Yes…"

"I want you very badly, Natalie. Not after five o'clock. Now," he told her, willing her to fall in with his demands. To let him bend her over the desk and take both of them where they were screaming with agony to go.

Canadian **Dani Collins** knew in high school that she wanted to write romance for a living. Twenty-five years later, after marrying her high school sweetheart, having two kids with him, working several generic office jobs and submitting countless manuscripts, she got 'The Call'. Her first Mills & Boon® Modern™ Romance won the Reviewers' Choice Award for Best First In Series from *RT Book Reviews*. She now works in her own office, writing romance.

SEDUCED INTO THE GREEK'S WORLD

BY
DANI COLLINS

MILLS &
BOON

Published in Great Britain 2015
by Mills & Boon, an imprint of Harlequin (UK) Limited,
Eton House, 18-24 Paradise Road, Richmond, Surrey, TW9 1SR

© 2015 Dani Collins

ISBN: 978-0-263-24878-4

Harlequin (UK) Limited's policy is to use papers that are natural, renewable and recyclable products and made from wood grown in sustainable forests. The logging and manufacturing processes conform to the legal environmental regulations of the country of origin.

Printed and bound in Spain
by CPI, Barcelona

SEDUCED
INTO THE
GREEK'S WORLD

To Cobe and Madison, who aren't with me
nearly enough, but were when I was writing this book.
xoxo Dani

CHAPTER ONE

HER LAUGH WAS so pure and spontaneous it caused Demitri Makricosta to look away from the Italian beauty flirting with him and seek out the source of the sound. As a connoisseur of fake laughter, often given to offering imitations himself, he found the naturalness of the woman's chuckle utterly engaging. It was feminine without being girlish or giggly, warm and sexy without being a put-on.

For a moment he didn't take in anything else but her. Short blond hair swung and fell as she tipped the precision cut backward. Her skin held a pale, translucent quality that made him think her cheek would feel cool but downy soft against his lips. He wondered how her skin smelled. Like summer fruit, maybe. Her profile was feminine and cute, right up to the tilt of her nose, while the rest of her was a study in mouthwatering curves.

Encased in a Makricosta uniform.

Damn, damn and damn.

The disappointment that flooded through him was surprisingly acute.

He took a more thorough tour of her uniform, wishing he didn't recognize it. It wasn't the pencil skirt and wispy red jacket over a bowed white top that the French staff wore here in Paris, which gave him a beat of hope. But if she'd been corporate, she'd have only a scarf or tie in company colors as part of her business ensemble.

Unfortunately, those long pants and the warm blazer

belonged to one of the Canadian outfits. The Makricosta
Elite in Montreal, if he wasn't mistaken—and he shouldn't
have any doubt because he had final say on every marketing decision in the family hotel chain right down to the
front-line image of the staff.

He didn't *want* to recognize it. That was the problem.
His male interest was seriously piqued by the woman wearing it.

Which wasn't like him. Women were fairly interchangeable for him. He never wondered, "Who is she? What's her
story?" Especially when he already had a female hand resting on his cuff and a voice murmuring, "*Bello?* What is it?"

"I thought I recognized someone," he prevaricated,
sending his companion a placating smile before glancing once more at the laughing woman—his employee—
across the lobby.

She was nodding at someone, tucking her hair coquett-
ishly behind her ear, saying something about email that
he read on her lips as noise from different sources echoed
across the foyer's marble floor and pillars.

Curious what kind of man was keeping that bright look
on her face, Demitri leaned back on the velvet settee, losing the touch of his prospective afternoon delight as he did.

Gideon.

Shock went through him as he recognized his brother-
in-law. Not that Gideon looked as though he was encouraging the woman, but Demitri still rose to his feet in brotherly
indignation. His sister had been through a lot, especially a
few years ago when Gideon's PA had intimated to Adara
that she and Gideon were having an affair. Demitri wasn't
going to sit here while some fresh tart made a play for
Adara's husband.

"I do recognize him," he stated grimly. "Excuse me."

But Gideon and the blonde were already parting ways
by the time he rounded the colonnade and approached.

The woman swung away with a brisk walk toward the front desk while Gideon glanced up in time to catch sight of Demitri. His expression hardened with determination.

That was when Demitri remembered he was avoiding the man.

"Good," Gideon stated as he approached. "I was going to find you before I left. Adara's birthday. You'll be there."

The eye to eye, man-to-man directive was annoying, but vaguely reassuring. Demitri liked seeing that Gideon was determined to make his wife happy. When that PA had set her sights on Gideon, Demitri had been on the verge of taking her for a tour himself to keep his sister's marriage intact. In the end, Gideon had salvaged his own marriage. He'd fired the woman before anything more than a few false and snarky claims had been made. Despite Adara's worries that Gideon was straying, in reality his devotion to her had never wavered and still appeared rock solid.

Which was good, Demitri supposed. He didn't wish any more strife on his sister than she'd already weathered, but she was so *annoyingly* happy. So determined to bring him into the fold of happily-ever-after she'd created for herself. The whole situation with his brothers and all their kids, the number of secrets kept from him... It grated in a way Demitri didn't like to dig into, so he slid his attention back to the blonde threatening his sister's happiness and latched on to ensuring she didn't try anything further with Gideon.

Better that than dealing with Gideon's demands.

"The date is in my calendar. I'll try to make it." Demitri dismissed him lightly.

Gideon folded his arms. His roots as a dock-rat sailor were visible in the piercing glint of his eyes. "Is there a reason you won't make it a priority?"

Given that Gideon had been part of the family for several years, Demitri didn't think he had to explain why these reunions Adara kept trying to organize were about as appealing to him as an impacted wisdom tooth.

"I'll do my best," he lied.

"Would you?" Gideon said flatly. The words *just for once* were silently tacked onto the end, loud and clear.

And here came Reason One why he had no desire to be around his family. *What are you doing with your life? Hold the baby. Isn't he adorable? When are you going to quit chasing skirts and settle down?*

Demitri mentally projected two words back at his brother-in-law, punctuated them with a tight smile before he walked away. Wasn't it enough that he had stepped up when Adara was pregnant? Hell, the only reason he'd gone into the family business was for her and Theo. Maybe he'd kept his own hours in the early years, but these days he showed up all the time, and kicked ass, if none of them had noticed. They could all play white picket fences with their new babies if they wanted to. He had zero interest in becoming a family man—and would make a terrible one—so they could all back the hell off.

Irritated, he glanced toward the Italian starlet watching him like a spaniel that had heard the car keys. As much as he would welcome the diversion of sex right now— lovemaking was his go-to coping strategy for any sort of tension—he was oddly disinterested in taking her upstairs. The blonde filled a bigger space in his mind, niggling at him.

Maybe she hadn't meant to cause this brief altercation with Gideon, but animosity toward her still bled into him like adrenaline. He wasn't so immature he couldn't figure out that he was blame shifting. Every time familial obligations tugged at him lately a wave of anger and rebellion came over him. Dark, miasmic thoughts sent him in search of self-destruction on one level or another.

Usually he subscribed to being a lover, not a fighter.

Forced himself to stay on the sane side of violence, too aware of the streak of it in his father. But nameless rage sat in him whenever he confronted the fact that his only real family, his brother and sister, the two people he trusted unequivocally, had kept him out of the loop on the existence of their eldest brother.

Had they not trusted him? Why had they cut him out like that? The betrayal sliced down the center of connection he felt toward them and pushed him out in the cold. If he didn't keep a lid on his emotions, his temper would mushroom out like a radiation cloud. It made for a lot of pressure. A cold, hard, dark feeling deep in his core that he refused to deconstruct, afraid of what he might find.

Instead, he channeled it into a wave of icy energy that carried him past the curious looks from the registration desk through to the administration offices, where he found the blonde Canadian in a chair cozily nudged up against the hotel manager's. The guy wasn't looking at where she pointed on the computer monitor. He was gazing down to where her breasts strained against the fabric of her shirt.

"I need to speak to you," Demitri said.

Natalie glanced up and felt the full impact of Demitri Makricosta, the youngest brother of the family that employed her. The one with the scandalously disreputable reputation. She'd seen him in person before, but always from a distance. Never like this, with his dark brown eyes pushing her back into her chair and then making a proprietary inspection of her buttons.

He was incredibly attractive. That fact was legendary across the hotel chain and impossible to ignore when he was barely ten feet away.

She tried comparing him to his older brother, Theo, who bore a resemblance but was more polished, kept a low profile and remembered every name and number he came across.

But there was no minimizing this man. All she could think was how Demitri was known for the wicked streak that was evident in his winged eyebrows and distant smile. Also for the women he picked up effortlessly, not to mention his utter disregard for little things like policies and procedures. Greek by birth but raised in America, he had a Mediterranean warmth to his skin tone under a shadow of stubble. He dressed like a citizen of the world in tailored pants and a suit vest buttoned over his shirt that accented his very fine shoulders and trim waist. He looked like the hottest of the 1920s gangsters.

Bad. He looked very, very bad. Full to the brim with sin.

She glanced up from taking him in and her gaze tangled with his. One of his superior brows went up in challenge of her checking him out. This was definitely a different kind of man from any she'd ever known. Sharp and far too knowing. How mortifying to be so obvious.

Decorum, Natalie. You're a mom.

Swallowing her discomfiture, she glanced at Monsieur Renault as she rose. A blush stung her cheeks.

"I'll go back to my office and you can call me when you're done. It's nice to meet you, Mr. Makricosta," she said as she approached the door, expecting him to move aside and give her a dismissive nod.

"It's you I want to talk to, Miss...?" He held out a hand.

Shock made her hesitate before she placed her hand in his and was jolted by the warm grip that enclosed hers. "Adams," she provided in a jagged, baffled voice. "Me? Are you sure?" Who did he think she was?

"I'm sure. Show me to your office." He released her and waved her into the hall.

Brushing past him and cooking in self-conscious warmth, she walked ahead of him down the narrow hall to her shared office. Her coworkers were away from their desks. That had been perfect at lunch when she'd connected with her daughter on one of her daily webcam calls. Zoey was having the time of her life with Grandma, not missing Natalie at all, which was a relief, but it still broke Natalie's heart. She'd shed a couple of tears after she'd disconnected, missing her girl dreadfully, and thankful for the privacy to do so. Now, however, her office mates' absence left an isolated mood in the small, musty-smelling room with its rain-blurred windows.

When he closed the door behind them, she felt as though all the oxygen was pulled out. "I'm not sure—?"

"Leave my brother-in-law alone," he said flatly.

"I— What?" The accusation was such a missile from the blue, she could only stare, insides flash-freezing. "Gideon? I mean, Mr. Vozaras?" she stammered.

"Gideon," he confirmed, but there was an underlying stealth to the word. As though he thought she was overstepping by using the man's name.

"What makes you think there's something going on between us?" She was so shocked she couldn't process how appalling the accusation was.

"I don't think there is. I know him and I know my sister, but I saw you flirting with him in the lobby, asking for his email. Back off or I'll have you fired."

"He showed me a photo of his son! The email is about work." Affront arrived, pushing into her face as a hot flush, straining her tone with the strident notes of the wrongly accused. "I don't go after married men! That's a disgusting thing to suggest. Especially when his wife was kind enough to give me this opportunity. That's the only reason he spoke to me at all. She asked him to pass along a message about a report she wants me to write. I said I hoped their son had got over his cold, and he showed me a photo of the boy after he'd found his way into the refrigerator."

The flicker of disdain that ticked in one of Demitri's

cheeks only infuriated her further, fueling her need to bring him down from his high horse.

"Who the hell are you to pass judgment anyway? Everything I've ever heard about your moral standards leaves me stunned and incredulous that you'd question mine."

That got his attention. His death glare gave her pause, but she was too outraged to stop.

"Oh, was that out of line? You don't think someone you only met seconds ago has the right to call you out? I thought rash personal comments were our special thing."

Okay, that did go too far. A hot blush flooded upward while she clenched her mouth shut. And folded her arms. And set her chin as she screwed up her courage to ask through her teeth, "*Are* you going to fire me?"

"For?" he prompted with a pithy look.

"Exactly," she shot out, unable to catch back the haughty response even though she was dying inside. She was so mad and embarrassed she couldn't even look at him. She liked this job. Needed it. The whole point in coming away on this assignment was to better her position in the organization. More compensation and responsibility translated to more stability and security for Zoey.

Yet here she was risking everything. What had possessed her to go off like that? Guilt? Because she'd secretly coveted Adara's doting husband, who so obviously loved his wife and child and supported them both in every possible way? Of course any woman would secretly wish she had that, but Natalie wasn't about to steal it to get it.

"What's your first name?" he asked.

"Natalie. Why?" She eyed him while keeping her face averted, half expecting him to pick up the phone to HR. Man, he was good-looking. And not the least bit ruffled. In fact, he almost looked as though he was laughing at her, which was so incensing she had to look away again.

"What are you doing here, Natalie? In Paris, I mean. What has Adara got you on? What's the special report?"

A chance to show off. Something she had imagined would help her take a step up the corporate ladder. So much for that. "I'm part of the software upgrade." It was hard to keep her voice steady as defensiveness and contrition pecked her. She kept it short. "I'm training the staff and working out the bugs. I've done Toulouse. I'm here in Paris for the week. Then I go to Lyon."

"You're an IT nerd?" His skepticism as he gave her another top-to-toe once-over was almost as irritating as the label.

"I wouldn't have guessed you're a marketing genius," she shot back, blithely matching his dismissive tone, thinking, *Stop it.* But he was so *infuriating.*

"A highly creative one," he assured smoothly. "Ask around. Although it sounds like you already have. You're doing all the hotels in Europe?"

"I—um, what?" That *creative* remark had thrown her, which had been his intention, she was sure. "No, I only have English and French and, um, can't be away longer than three weeks."

She and Zoey wouldn't starve if he fired her, she reminded herself. The knowledge calmed her nerves. She wouldn't even lose her house, and she always had the fallback plan of moving in with her ex-mother-in-law, which would suit Zoey just fine because she loved the farm. She'd been beside herself that she would stay with her grandma for three weeks. No, this was a minor, very awkward speed bump that Natalie would get over as quickly as possible.

"I've always wanted to travel, so…" She cleared her throat as she realized that was too much information and headed back to bare facts. "They're trying to implement before the end of the year. There's a whole team. One person couldn't do it all."

"So you're here to work and see the sights. Not have an affair. That's what you're telling me?"

"Yes." From somewhere deep in her subconscious, a fresh blush rose. "Of course I'm here to work." Maybe she had thought this trip was her chance to have a grown-up affair away from her daughter's impressionable eyes, but that was very much a midnight fantasy and not something she intended to pursue. This trip might be the opportunity to cast off responsibility and act like a single woman instead of a struggling mom with bills and a flake for an ex, but she'd settle for a date with someone she wouldn't have met otherwise.

He didn't need to know any of that though.

Her cheeks stayed hot and hurting, nevertheless. It wasn't easy to meet his gaze and pretend a full-fledged affair was completely off the table, especially when there was a knowing glint teasing crinkles into the corners of his eyes.

"Even if I was looking for romance," she blurted. "Which I'm *not*, I'd hardly start with the owner of the company, would I?"

"I don't know. Would you? Let's have dinner tonight and talk about it."

Her stomach swooped and her heart stopped, as though she'd hit an unexpected wall.

That's how it's done. She'd been observing, trying to crack the code of dating and casual invitations. It had seemed complicated, but he made it look easy.

Practice, she surmised cynically.

But go out with him? *Impossible.* Her heart restarted, pounding with sudden panic, partly because, well, look at him. He was gorgeous and obviously knew his way around the entire city, not just the block.

Danger. If she could have escaped this airless room crowded with empty desks, she would have.

Somehow she managed to hang on to her composure and scoff, "Is that a test? I realize Theo— And yes, at this level we all refer to your family by your first names when you're not around to hear it." She encompassed the ground floor with a sweep of her splayed hand in a flat circle. "*Theo* might have married a woman who once worked as a chambermaid, but we're all well aware that was an exception. *I* have no such ambitions. You're quite safe from me, and so are the rest of the men in your family."

There. She folded her arms to close the topic.

He folded his, bunching those gorgeous shoulders in a way that made her throat go dry. "You're funny," he said.

"I'm completely serious!"

"I know. That's why it's funny. Calling marriage to any of us an ambition is hysterical." He didn't laugh. He only gave his mouth an ironic twist, which drew her notice to the shape of his lips. The lower was fuller than the top one, but the upper had a shallow space between the two peaks, perfect for a fingertip. The corners of his mouth extended into short, deep lines that gave him that look of being perpetually amused by the lives of the mortals around him.

His smile grew and he jerked his chin in a nudge of insistence, voice pitched intimately low, filled with knowledge that she was responding to him. "Have dinner with me, Natalie."

She was *mooning*. And he'd noticed. Of course he had. He was a serial pickup artist. Where were the natural disasters when you needed them? It was definitely time for the earth to open up and suck her underground.

"Dating among coworkers is frowned upon," she managed, delighted to have found both the excuse and a steady voice. "I'm sorry you thought I was making a play for your brother-in-law, but I'm highly cognizant of company policy and have no intention of violating it, even if he were available. Now, if we're finished, I really should get back to work."

"You're sorry for my mistake? This really is the beginning of a beautiful friendship. Come on. Dinner. It will be my apology." He splayed his straight fingers against his wide chest. A gorgeous chest, she was sure. He looked like he worked out. Often. His physique distracted her from how suddenly he'd turned on the charm. "Where's the harm in the boss taking an out-of-town employee to dinner? It's networking," he cajoled.

"Is that what it would be?" She couldn't help her snort of laughter. She'd thought he was merely a playboy, but he made the sharing of his favors sound like some kind of a job perk.

His expression changed slightly as she laughed, becoming less arrogant as his regard sharpened with male interest and something more acute, as though he was reassessing her. It made her think she might be holding her own in this match of wits, surprising him.

Which gave her a thrill that she did her best to ignore.

"Look, I'm flattered," she rushed to say, glancing away so he wouldn't see *how* flattered. As sophisticated as she dreamed of being, she wasn't prepared for someone like him. "But I've seen the women you date and I'm not in their league. Which, by the way, is another reason I would never set my sights on your brother-in-law. So thank you for this extremely interesting conversation, but I need to get back to work. I don't want to get fired," she added pointedly.

"Not in their league?" he repeated, frowning in disagreement as he gave her yet another thorough assessment in a way that set her alight. Her entire body actually hurt from the blood rush that prickled through her.

She'd starved herself and worked out like mad before leaving Montreal, determined that if any sort of corporate limelight fell upon her—or any sexy Frenchmen—she'd have nothing to be insecure about. Nevertheless, she experienced a pang of insecurity under his review, worried she wasn't up to standard.

He dragged his gaze back up to hers and let her see undisguised male desire.

Tingling excitement encompassed her. It wasn't exactly confidence, but it wasn't uncertainty, either. It was a delicious and involuntary "yes, please" that scared the hell out of her.

"You're very much in an elite league of your own, Natalie. Or are you making excuses to spare my feelings? It would surprise me if you are. You don't strike me as someone who would bother. Not considering the frankness we've already arrived at."

That made her chuckle drily, but she suppressed it with a sheepish dip of her chin. "You're right. But read my personnel file, Mr. Makricosta—"

"Demitri," he corrected.

"I don't live nearly as fast as you do. Demitri." She tried to make her voice diffident and amused, but Demitri was a surprisingly erotic name for a man with an American accent. "If I thought you were issuing a genuine invitation—and one that was only for dinner," she added with a you-can't-fool-me look. "I would be tempted. My coworkers here have families to go home to. It would be refreshing not to eat alone. But I suspect you're mocking me. Or maybe punishing me for said frankness?"

He was taken aback by that. "Why wouldn't I want to take you out? You're beautiful, amusing and you have a pretty laugh."

The sincerity in his tone made her heart swing inside her chest, dipping and lifting in a way that made her set a hand on the edge of her desk for balance. She grappled for humor to deflect how thoroughly his simple compliment disarmed her.

"And you want to hear that laugh in bed?" she challenged.

"Ha!" His chuckle was surprised and real, his grin appreciative before it turned hot and hungry. His gaze closed around her like a fist.

"I'll have the car brought to the curb for seven."

CHAPTER TWO

Don't bother.

That was all she'd had to say before he had winked and left her alone in her office. She could have chased him down, although she'd kept her eye out for him the rest of the day, filled with misgivings, but hadn't seen him. The intercompany email was the simplest option. It didn't even require the awkwardness of explaining herself. All she would have had to type was I can't make it.

She hadn't.

Why not?

Oh, she'd come up with dozens of rationalizations including, "it's only dinner." She was lonely and homesick. Travel for work wasn't as glamorous as she'd expected, especially without someone to share stories with, and calling Zoey twice a day wasn't nearly enough. She was used to her daughter disappearing for a weekend with her father up to the farm, but going on ten days without being able to hug her girl was a form of slow torture.

Therefore, she reasoned, she was entitled to a night out on the company that had separated them. She'd already put in tons of extra hours on this project. She and Demitri would probably talk about work anyway. She certainly wasn't looking at this as a real date. Definitely not one where she might get lucky.

She shaved her legs anyway. Then put on the sexy black underwear she'd bought here in Paris and topped it with a black lace sheath over a black slip. She stepped into the heels she'd picked up at the consignment store before leaving Montreal, the ones she'd debated whether to bring at all because they were too high to be practical for anything less than a night on the town. With her fake diamond earrings winking from behind the fall of her freshly washed hair and her makeup more dramatic than usual, she was as date-worthy as she'd ever been.

Then she stood at the curb like an idiot for ten minutes.

Wow. What a prince. And she had developed quite a jerk radar after her brief marriage and lengthy attempt to finalize her divorce. Well, she'd wanted a taste of the dating scene. Who knew it was this bitter? But it was exactly this well-honed resentment of thoughtless men that steeled her spine and made her demand better for herself whenever she had offers back home.

Pivoting to go back inside the hotel, she entered the rotating doors as Demitri entered them from the inside. She ignored him as she passed him and kept walking into the lobby.

"Hey!" he circled back to call after her. "Natalie. Wait."

"I was stood up," she said over her shoulder, then paused to swing around and level a glare at him. "Lesson learned. If that was your intention. Good night." She swung back toward the elevators.

"I stood at your door thinking the same thing."

She checked her step. Turned to search his expression. He looked annoyed, not smug or smarmy. She didn't want to believe him, too aware that giving men the benefit of the doubt was an invitation to be walked over.

"You said to meet you at the curb," she reminded him coolly. Her entire body prickled with awareness that the front desk and bell staff could see them, if not hear them.

"No, I said the car would be there." He came even with

her and scowled. "What kind of men have you dated that they pick you up on the sidewalk?"

That gave her pause. For all her ideals, she still expected the very worst from men. Maybe she ought to give Demitri more credit.

He offered his arm, gaze still vaguely hostile.

After a brief hesitation, she transferred her pocketbook to her other hand and tucked her fingers into the crook of his elbow, nervous now because she wasn't sure how to take him. Was he one of the few good ones after all?

With *his* reputation?

He skimmed a glance down her front to where her dress was revealed by her open raincoat. "I'll forgive you for underestimating me since you look so lovely," he commented.

It wasn't the most extravagant compliment, kind of backhanded in the way he suggested she was seeking his forgiveness, but she warmed under his words. And couldn't help taking a visual snapshot of him in his black pants and black buttoned shirt under a smoky gray suede jacket that was so buttery soft it made her want to caress his arm. He smelled fantastic, too, all spicy and masculine, jaw shiny where he'd freshly shaved.

They turned more than a few heads walking out to the car, but she doubted it was because they made such a striking couple. She'd have to make a point of mentioning how innocuous this evening had been when training her coworkers over the next few days. He'd been just being nice, she'd stress. Even though she doubted a man like Demitri went out of his way to be nice. She suspected he was ruled by self-interest, and most of his interest was banked below his belt.

For the moment, however, she set all that aside and concentrated on not smiling like an idiot because she was on a date. With a handsome man. This was exactly what she'd hoped for from this off-site assignment, and it astonished her that it was happening. Her neglected femininity had been desperate for male attention and glowed with pleasure at getting some.

They didn't talk much in the limo. Her fault as she took in the color and lights of Paris. The restaurant was only a short drive anyway, a distance she would have walked in Montreal, even in this blustery fall weather and wearing these neck-breaking shoes. They were shown to a table with a stunning view of Notre Dame and the Seine. She tried not to gawk as they moved through the dining room, but along with gorgeous detailing that spoke of France's rich history, the place was loaded with movie stars. There were probably athletes and politicians, too, not that she would recognize them. Demitri seemed to have a nodding acquaintance with almost everyone in the room, but didn't stop to speak to anyone.

"Shall I order for you?" he asked as the maître d' left them.

"What kind of men have I dated that dared to let me read the menu myself? As if a woman could," she scoffed lightly.

"This is why I asked. Some of you feminists find it condescending."

"And you see it as chivalry?"

"I had an old-world upbringing," he stated with a ring of pride in his tone. "But I also like to know my date is ordering something I'd like to eat, since she won't finish it," he added with a supercilious lift at the corner of his mouth.

"Ha! You don't know me very well, do you?"

"I'm working on it," he assured her with a look that reached across and held.

"You read my personnel file?" she challenged, heart skipping. He knew about Zoey? Her breath stopped.

"Too easy," he dismissed, leaning forward in a way that seemed to catch her in a magnetic field that pulled her into him. "I like a more personal approach."

So he didn't know she had a daughter. Natalie toyed with the idea of blurting it out, but didn't want to cool the sizzle between them. It was too exciting, playing with this particular fire.

"I'll bet you do." Her voice came out papery and soft. He probably knocked women over with gently blown kisses. Her pulse was racing and her skin glowing hot from the inside. The way the banter lobbed back and forth between them entranced her, but he was an expert, she reminded herself. This wasn't anything so grand as chemistry.

"If you think I'm such a womanizer, why are you here?" he asked, eyes narrowed to hide what he was thinking.

"Honestly?" She schooled herself not to look or sound desperate, even though she was bordering on despair where men and relationships were concerned. "I live like a shut-in, working from home a lot of the time. I'll never get another chance to dine like the one percent and, quite frankly, you hit the nail on the head about the men I date. I thought I'd see what it's like to be the girl for a change."

He raised his brows.

"Let you hold the door for me," she explained. "Pay. Even though I know it'll really be the company paying. But you do know this is only dinner, right? I work for you."

"You work for my brother," he stated firmly, not thrown off his stride at all by her bluntness. "IT falls under finance. I head up marketing." Despite his affable tone his gaze was dead level as he added, "My threats earlier were empty. I have no authority to fire you. By the same token, I have no way of helping you advance. If this turns into more than dinner, there's no professional advantage for you."

The warning pushed her back into her seat, putting her in her place. Yet she was strangely relieved. Embarrassed, yet amused.

"Look at all we've got on the table and we haven't even ordered," she said with a pert lift of her brows.

* * *

Demitri released a "Ha," and looked away, astounded by how thoroughly this woman was keeping him on his toes. Fortunately the waiter arrived to advise them of the evening's specials.

"Please," Natalie said when Demitri glanced at her. "Order for me. I'm curious."

He nodded in satisfaction even though his brain was barely able to pull it together to order at all, only managing to choose the starters with a suitable wine before he turned back to her, trying not to fall into her spell like a fisherman off a boat.

When had she hooked him? That first laugh? The doe-eyed virgin look when he'd asked to speak to her? Definitely by the time she'd cut him down to size with a few swings of her rapier tongue, he'd been curious. Everyone loved him. Instantly and thoroughly. Even his family only acted irritated as they made every effort to draw him further inside the fold. Hell, women he slept with and left within hours remained affectionate and syrupy when he crossed paths with them later.

But not Natalie. He didn't think it was an act, either. She'd been furious and insulted by his accusations today, then mistrustful and apprehensive of his invitation to dinner. When she hadn't answered her door, he'd been stunned. No one rejected him, no matter what he did. And he searched for the line at every opportunity.

Finding her at the front of the hotel had been entirely too much of a relief for his comfort. Then she'd demonstrated that she was perfectly ready to leave him in the dust for being thoughtless. The warning lights were still flashing. Off her and inside him.

Only dinner, she'd claimed.

Take heed, he told himself. He avoided women with

standards, being genetically incapable of living up to anything but the basest expectations of him.

Her honesty and playfulness were incredibly refreshing, however. And she was beautiful, with that skin like creamed honey and her eyes reflecting the sparkling lights from beyond the window.

"Tell me about yourself, Natalie," he commanded softly.

Something like indecision passed over her face before she brought her gaze around to his. Her expression smoothed to an aloof facade, as though she'd mentally tucked away everything personal and only left the basics.

"There's not much to say. I grew up outside of Montreal with my mother and brother. I divorced pretty much as soon as I married and worked on contract with Makricosta for two years before I was hired for a permanent position with the Canadian branch. Sometimes I go on-site across the country, but most of what I do is handled over the phone and through screen-share from my home office."

"Turn it off and turn it on again?" he guessed.

"Exactly. Along with some talking off the ledge when files are corrupted or a job change demands a revision of an email signature and they can't find where to update it. The excitement in tech support never stops, let me tell you. I couldn't figure out why my ear felt weird the first few days I was in France and finally realized it's because I wasn't wearing my Bluetooth."

There was more, he suspected, but before he could dig, she turned his inquiry around. "You?"

"Why don't you tell me what you know? Through your carefully vetted research," he drawled, and liked the way her full lips pursed in compunction. He wasn't bothered. Of course the employees gossiped about him. He made about as much effort to be discreet as he did toward curbing misbehavior overall. The whole point was to let his escapades be known in order to reach maximum exasperation factor.

Which was juvenile, he realized, reflecting on it under Natalie's regard and feeling the first traces of shame, but he had his reasons for making himself the target of attention.

"I don't actually know that much," Natalie said. "Your family keeps a low profile. Your brother turning up with a baby with the chambermaid was a hot topic for a while, but since I don't work directly in the hotels, I don't have close friendships with anyone at work and only get the odd bits of gossip fed back to me. There are some people I talk to all the time, and when I'm solving a crisis I'm very popular, but mostly I'm regarded as a necessary evil. Right now, making all these changes to the main system? It's a good thing I have a thick skin because I'm not anyone's friend. Which sounds like I'm talking about myself again. What a bore I am!"

"I'm interested," he assured her, surprised by how true the comment was. "How old were you when you married?"

"Not old enough," she said with a circumspect lift of her lashes. "Nineteen. Have you ever been married?"

"Hell, no."

"Wish I'd had your sense." The wry curl at the corner of her mouth and couched bitterness behind her eyes suggested she was being completely forthright.

A woman after my own heart, he thought ironically.

"What happened to cut your marriage short? Infidelity?" Hell, at that age he had broken up his brother's impending marriage, coldly and deliberately.

Natalie didn't answer right away. Her lips pursed in old disappointment as she stared out the window. "The short answer is he didn't come to my mother's funeral," she finally allowed.

When she swung her face back to him, it was as if she was saying, *There. I did it.* As if her telling him without showing too much emotion had been very hard.

A weird, answering pain lurched in his chest.

He was a student of human behavior. People thought he was superficial and lacking in empathy. He was fine with the misconception. Deep thoughts really didn't interest him, but he was very good at reading people. Years of living in a house where emotions were so deeply hidden you needed a pickax to find them had honed his skills. The side benefit was that it made him good at his job. Good with women.

Natalie didn't want his sympathy, however. The keep-away vibes rolling off her were obvious and troubling. Especially because, for once, he knew exactly how she felt.

"I couldn't face my mother's funeral alone. I brought a date. How twisted is that?" he confided.

"Adara and Theo weren't there?"

"No, they were." And Nic, the older brother Demitri hadn't known about. He averted his mind from how disturbing it had been to have a stranger enter their inner circle, as though a member of the audience had walked on stage and begun acting with the players, throwing off his lines. "We're not close in a way that would have made something like that easier." He'd barely spoken to them at all, too stunned and filled with questions he refused to ask.

"But you said you grew up with your mother and brother, so he must have been at the funeral with you?"

She flinched and sat back, distancing herself even more. She straightened her silverware and looked quite pale despite the golden glow of candlelight on her skin.

"He died the year before. Can we not talk about this please?"

"I'm sorry." When had he ever been so aghast at stepping on someone's feelings? Or apologized so sincerely to a woman? But his hand was over hers before he knew he was going to reach out to make a connection. "Really. Theo drives me bat-guano-crazy, but I don't know what I'd do without him."

She laughed. It was more of a sniff, and she brushed at her cheek, eyes wet and glowing when she lifted them. "Thank you. It was six years ago, but I still miss him and think about him every day."

The waiter arrived to distract them. By the time they were alone again, Natalie had her bravest smile back in place. "Tell me why your brother drives you crazy."

He shook his head. "You'll have *me* in tears," he dismissed.

"Your job, then. Will you talk about that?"

"You can't be interested," he deflected. Where were questions like "Were you in Cannes for the festival?" "Where do you summer?"

Natalie shrugged. "I'm certainly not interested in myself. This is the most excitement I've had in my life. True story," she assured him with a confirming nod. "You travel, at least. Meet famous people."

"People who think they're famous are boring as hell. *That* is a true story. But come on. You must have at least one deep, dark secret that makes you interesting."

"One," she allowed promptly, suppressing a smile. "But it's not very dark. Dirty blond at best. And I'm not going to tell you." She had decided that, since this was her one chance to act like a carefree young woman instead of a mom. It was harmless, she told herself. This was only dinner.

"I want to hear it," he insisted.

She shook her head, firm. "You'll think differently of me. But what about you? Any dark secrets falling out of your pockets?"

His guard was so low he almost told her about Nic. The fact his siblings had kept the man's existence from him had completely unraveled his view of his life and his place in the family. The exclusion had rocked his foundation, and he'd begun mentally separating from them, thinking more seriously about starting his own marketing firm.

Gideon had called a few weeks later to announce Adara's pregnancy and to inform Demitri that he would be expected to step up and take on extra hours in the family business. Demitri had been needed again. Integral to the business and to his sister. Things had gone back to normal for a while, but then Adara had started trying to get everyone together. She and Theo were as thick as thieves with their parenthood jokes, and he was once again on the outside looking in.

They weren't even leaning on him at work anymore. Quite the opposite, which was eating at his sense of self. With practiced ease he turned his mind from all of that, distracting Natalie with some of his stock stories that always drew a laugh. He knew loads of celebrities and had made a career of partying with them. His siblings had certainly never loosened up enough to ensure their highest-paying guests had fun.

That was Demitri's job: creating distraction. Drawing and holding attention.

Natalie was rapt, thoroughly engaged with everything he told her. It wasn't a strange occurrence for him. Everyone, women especially, responded to him. He'd recognized it early and used it to this day. The difference tonight was how much he enjoyed her attention while at the same time resenting that she wanted him to talk when he wanted to hear more about her.

They lingered over their meal, finishing the bottle of wine and nursing coffee, steering away from personal topics in favor of movies and news scandals and places he'd been that she'd like to visit.

"You're a single woman. Get on a plane," he ordered. "What's holding you back?"

"I did get on a plane," she argued good-naturedly, shielding her eyes with a downward sweep of her lashes. "I'm here. Dining on the Seine. Thank you for a lovely evening," she added, flashing her gaze back up to his. "This is what I'd hoped for when I applied for this trip."

She'd been looking for a man to seduce her. He could see it and a pulse of sexual excitement pumped through him. But seduction required patience, he reminded himself.

"Do you like dancing? We could go to a club."

"I... It's a work night," she argued, but the slant of her gaze told him she was tempted.

He smirked. "I begin to see why you don't have a life." He signaled for the check.

"Note to self—boss thinks a work ethic is overrated," she chirped.

"I'm not your boss," he reminded. "C'mon. I know you want to tick the box on dance in a Paris nightclub."

"Yes, but..." She canted her head at him, nose wrinkled. "I'm not dressed for it."

"Believe me, truly cool people do not dress for clubs. They drop in on impulse."

"And get turned away at the door for not being on the list."

"You're adorable. I'm *always* on the list."

She had definitely had one glass too many if she was teetering into not giving a damn about work or propriety, but Demitri was a difficult man to say no to. He took her hand and wound her through the restaurant, tucking her into the back of the limo and angling his body so he looked at her the whole way to the club.

"This is a bad idea," she insisted, trying desperately to hang on to a few grains of common sense while turning a challenging look on him that only clicked into a locked gaze with his.

His grin widened. "Because it's turning into more than dinner?"

"You're the kind of man who always gets what he wants, aren't you?"

"Yes," he answered without reserve.

Be careful, Natalie. Be very, very careful.

"Well, I'm only going along out of curiosity," she excused with a toss of her hair. "Don't say I led you on. Oh, we won't even get in," she added as they pulled up at the entrance where a hundred people stood in the rain, all dressed to the nines.

He made a pithy noise and waited until the chauffeur had opened the door and held an umbrella for them, walking them to the door.

"Jean," Demitri greeted the doorman, slipping him a bill without even pausing.

Pounding music accosted them as they entered the dark interior. Flashes of neon pierced the violet glow while strips of white stood out in stark contrast. As they wound through the crowded tables and bouncing bodies, a stunning woman with a lot of dark skin exposed by her French maid inspired two-piece bikini lowered her serving tray and kissed both of Demitri's cheeks. They had a brief conversation, she pointed, he nodded and then he tugged Natalie along with him as they continued toward the back of the club.

He said something into her ear, but she must have heard him wrong. She looked to the stage, but that DJ couldn't be the pop star he'd just mentioned.

Maybe it was, though. A chart-topping band occupied the VIP section and rose to greet Demitri with exuberance when he arrived, insisting they join their entourage, which included a dozen people, three of whom she recognized, two from television and one from a blockbuster movie.

More champagne was ordered and she was pressed into a chair next to a movie star.

Oh, sweet Lord. What kind of life had she stepped into that she was partying in Paris with celebrities? No wonder women dropped like flies for Demitri. He plucked them out of their boring little lives and set them into fantasy worlds where money wasn't mentioned and rich, gorgeous men flattered you shamelessly.

Not that she felt the same frisson of awareness and excitement when this very handsome actor leaned in to fawn over her, but the way he kept asking her about herself, as though he was genuinely interested, was enormously gratifying to her small-time ego. When he asked her to dance, of course she said yes. What a story to tell her grandchildren! *I once danced in Paris with a movie star.*

He was a bit handsy in real life. Drunk, she assumed. Not outright offensive but awfully familiar awfully fast. He wanted to dance right up against her and she told herself to go with it. This was how the high rollers lived, right on the edge, she supposed. And honestly, if she wanted to flirt with a wealthy stranger, this guy was probably a far simpler entanglement than Demitri.

He roamed his hands over her hips, skewing her dress up her thighs and she let him, hoping for a flicker of the physical spark she felt with Demitri.

An arm shot between them, separating her from the actor and none too gently forcing the man back.

Demitri stepped into the space he'd created, his posture one of startling aggression even though he said nothing, only stood there like a wall between her and the movie star.

"I thought you were done with her," the actor excused, holding up his hands.

Oh, *yuck.* Instantly feeling worthless and dirty, Natalie turned away.

Her arm was caught in a hard grip and Demitri said next to her ear, "We're leaving."

You think? she wanted to snap, but didn't bother. She was so offended and disgusted she wanted to evaporate. Maybe she owned some responsibility for that ugly remark since she hadn't exactly been discouraging the actor. Even so, it didn't excuse his talking about her as though she was something to be picked up and passed around. She wasn't an object.

And what did that say about Demitri that his women moved through the ranks?

And, if that was normal behavior for him, why was he acting all possessive? Because he hadn't actually had her yet? What if she'd been into that other guy? He didn't have to come on like he owned her, escorting her to the car as though he'd just bailed her out of jail. Giving her a shoulder of glacial ice because she'd danced with his friend.

"You know…" she began over the sound of the tires hissing through the wet streets.

"Not right now," he said in a deadly tone.

Seriously? She glared at his incredibly still posture, eyes facing front, jaw set, hands in loose fists on his thighs. As the silence thickened, she realized that hissing sound was his breath moving in measured soughs through his flared nostrils.

That signal of barely controlled fury gave her pause when she really wanted to rail at him. He'd set her up to be hit on and now he was mad it had happened, as though it was her fault. They drove in silence until they reached the hotel. As they entered the lobby, she said frostily, "Don't bother walking me to my room. Thanks for dinner."

"Suit yourself," he said through his teeth, and walked toward the elevators.

She stared at his back, brain throbbing with the knowledge it was better to leave it like this, him going to his room where everyone could see she was *not* following.

But she still needed to take the elevator to her own room.

Her feet carried her in swift clips of her heels across the marble until she was right beside him.

"I'm a free agent," she whispered. "In case you missed the part about this evening not coming with any guarantees. So how about you knock off acting as if I'm a tease who bruised your ego by dancing with your best friend."

Demitri slowly turned his head and watched her eyes widen like a gopher realizing she'd called down a raptor and was being swallowed by its shadow. Her throat worked and she pulled her elbows in against her body, telling him exactly how menacing he must look. But even though he was holding himself firmly in check, he couldn't shake the fury that had lit in him with a gasoline-fueled *whoosh* when he'd glanced over and seen that Natalie was gone.

Finding her on the dance floor being pawed by that overpaid puppet had further infuriated him, making an unfamiliar phrase explode in his head: *She's mine.*

He'd watched himself from a distance behaving like a jealous lover, unable to countenance where this streak of possessiveness had come from, but his desire to do violence had been disturbingly strong.

Especially when he'd heard the actor's tasteless comment.

Natalie's recoil had been a visceral stab to his gut, making him see how he was tarnishing someone nowhere near as cynical and jaded as he was. He'd been instantly disgusted with himself.

"Is that what you think? That I'm angry with *you*?" The skin across his cheekbones felt tight and he heard how low and chilling his voice was, coming from a churning, ugly place deep in his chest. "We had to leave, Natalie, because I was going to kill him."

The elevator doors opened, but neither of them moved. She stared into his eyes and he let her see the banked rage burning in his.

The doors started to close, and he shot out a hand to catch them back. Waving her into the car, he leaned in and pressed the button. "Good night."

"Wait," she insisted, holding the doors herself from the inside. "I probably kind of let him think—"

"No, you didn't," he said flatly. "I did." And he was so filled with self-contempt, with *shame*, he didn't know how to deal with it.

"What?"

He looked away, regretting he'd said anything. But he couldn't let her think he was calling her out for drawing that man's attention when he was the one who'd put her in the actor's line of sight in the first place.

Inhaling to gather his composure, he stepped into the elevator and punched the button for the penthouse, folding his arms and bracing his feet as he faced her. The elevator began to climb.

"I don't typically care if the women I take to these things choose to leave with someone else. That guy knows it. Hell, most of the women I date come on to me for an introduction to a crowd like that. *I don't care*," he insisted, because until this evening, he genuinely hadn't.

"But tonight you did?" She was very somber, looking up at him with something that approached concern. As though she sensed he was facing a demon, which was as painful as actually looking into the hard light of self-reflection.

"Tonight I saw how tawdry it is," he acknowledged.

The elevator stopped at her floor, making her take a half step for balance. The doors opened, but they stayed in the suspended elevator, the air so thick with tension it held no oxygen.

"He embarrassed me," Demitri admitted, teeth locked and trying to hold in the uncomfortable revelation. "He made me embarrassed of myself. You said you weren't in the same league as the women I usually date, and that's true."

She flinched, taken aback.

"You're well beyond anything they could aspire to," he expounded. "Not as worldly, I'll give you that, but you have the kind of standards the people I call friends wouldn't even begin to understand."

"That's not true," she argued. Glancing out to the hall, she motioned that he should release the door. She seemed embarrassed, as though she wanted privacy.

As he allowed the doors to close again, she clasped her hands before her, shoulders hunched and defensive, brow crinkled and looking mortified.

The elevator began the rest of its climb.

"I'm not worldly, that's dead-on. But I don't have any kind of great standards. I came to France kind of fantasizing about having an affair, just like you accused me this afternoon. I mean, obviously not really expecting anything to happen," she stammered, wringing her hands. "But as I was dancing, I was letting myself think it could. I'm sure I gave him the wrong impression."

His brain went supernova, exploding in his head, sweeping out any other thought but that he could have her.

"If you want an affair, Natalie, I'm your man." His voice plummeted into throaty depravity, the want in him so quick and intense it tightened his airway.

Her lashes quivered and her pupils expanded. "I… It was just a fantasy," she insisted—voice, tone, protest thin and insubstantial.

The elevator stopped again.

He pinned the door automatically with the well-practiced step of his foot into the sensor and the rest of him in her space.

She was off balance, breasts rising in a startled gasp as her hand went behind her, searching blindly for the rail.

He braced his hands against the wall on either side of her head and took his time gazing on her wary expression, letting her get used to the idea. Some primal part of him deliberately forgot why he'd meant to let her go home alone.

"The first time I saw you I thought you would have such soft skin." He leaned close enough to draw in the scent of her flushed cheek, letting their body heat build in the tiny space he allowed between them. Seduction was about giving a woman time to feel the want, then providing the relief.

"I'm not sure," she whispered, but her gaze was on his mouth. Yearning parted her lips. "I didn't mean for you to think…"

Patience, he warned himself, practically trembling with the avalanche of desire building behind his wall of self-control.

"I want this…" she whispered.

He moved in with the skill of a man who always got what he wanted, not by force, but persuasion.

Her mouth was a tender morsel that made his breath hiss out in gratification as he nuzzled it with his own. She responded hesitantly, then with openness, inviting his full possession, letting him guide her toward the sensual world he longed to explore with her. She was delightful, shy yet generous, eyes closed tight in pained pleasure. When a little sob of capitulation left her, when she brought her hands from behind her back to his chest and splayed them in a promising caress, he drew back just enough to speak.

"Come with me."

CHAPTER THREE

DON'T, SHE THOUGHT.

But in the back of her mind, she asked herself, *What's holding you back?* She had mentally allowed for something like this to happen. Heck, she'd actually bought condoms, thinking at the time that it was a ridiculous prospect, but secretly dreaming of being swept off her feet by a suave foreigner. Demitri was a prime example of the sophisticated man she'd hoped to meet. Plus, he actually knew how these situations worked.

But she hadn't expected an affair to actually happen. She was normal, boring, run-of-the-mill Natalie. Not some irresistible, exciting woman who captivated a man.

Demitri looked at her as if she was that and more. He made her feel beautiful and alluring, as though she was the kind of woman who deserved a man to love and cherish her. That fantasy was as seductive as the genuine tingles of arousal he provoked in her.

When he closed his hand around hers and backed out of the elevator, drawing her with him, she let it happen.

Knees weak, heart pounding, lips still burning, she allowed him to lead her down the hallway, half convinced this was a dream because things like this didn't really happen. Not to her.

They passed recessed doors that led to private suites. She'd only been in one Makricosta penthouse ever, to resolve a Wi-Fi issue for a client she hadn't even seen. She knew *of* the family suites in each of the hotels, but hadn't ever expected to see the interior of one.

Demitri let her in a door marked Private Residence.

She took in the overstuffed semicircle couch and round coffee table, the dining area and table for twelve, the marble mantel and matching accent tables. Table lamps provided soft light against the draped windows. The art on the walls looked expensive. The suite was tasteful and welcoming, if cold. Not as generic as a hotel room, but not really lived in.

"Take your coat?" he offered.

She set her pocketbook on the chest beside the door and offered her back, nerves strummed by the brush of his fingertips as he lowered her coat off her shoulders. The brush of silk lining down her arms caused her to shiver, making her nipples pull tight. Everything in her tensed with anticipation while nerves had her heart hammering in her throat.

Was she really doing this? She ought to tell him that she didn't do this. It wasn't her. He'd be disappointed.

Working up her courage, she turned, hands clasped before her.

He was looking at her legs, coat suspended from his hand. As she turned, he lifted his gaze to hers, locking her in a heated stare, not looking away as he tossed her wet coat toward the leather sofa.

"You shouldn't do that," she protested, taking an automatic step to fetch it.

He stepped into her space. The air between them thinned like smoke, leaving a vacuum that pulled them into the space, energy sizzling and popping with sexual awareness.

He was so gorgeous. Not just that sculpted jaw and his intense dark eyes, but the kissable shape of his lips and the scope of his shoulders. His wide chest and flat abdomen and long legs.

I don't know what I'm doing. She tried to find the words, tried to make her throat work, but he touched a fingertip under her chin.

The brush was feathery and gentle. She hadn't expected finesse, but honestly, a man didn't rack up a conquest list like his by being a brute. He was showing her all his best moves, she reminded herself, but she still felt deliciously branded by his fingerprint. Lifting her gaze, she wound up fascinated by his mouth again, and it was coming closer...

Oh.

When had she even been *kissed* since having Zoey? Really kissed?

And so well?

He really knew what he was doing, persuading her with varying pressures and parted lips to follow him. Open. Let it deepen. Rock and soothe and moan involuntarily because it felt so good.

Seductive.

His arm hooked behind her and drew her into the hard wall of his chest. *So* good. And why? Why did the sheer hardness of him, the tension of strong muscles and flat breastbone and firm flesh, make her soften and weaken and melt into surrender?

So much strength harnessed and held in check for her.

He stroked his hands up and down her spine and she kept leaning closer and more fully, giving up more of herself until she was plastered to him, completely undone. Then he slid one hand down to clasp over her buttock and a heated zing of pleasure pierced deep in her belly, sending a flood of sexual awakening into her erogenous zones.

This was what she'd wanted. Sexual feelings. Womanly feelings. To be seduced so she wouldn't have to think about right and wrong. Grateful to him for making this easy, she wound her arms around his neck and licked into his mouth, letting him know she was utterly receptive.

He grunted, hips jerking into her in a way that spoke of his excitement, which excited her in turn. With a bolder touch, he cupped her backside and found her breast, possessed it, stimulated her through the fabric of her dress so she wriggled against him with impatient desire.

They were breathing heavily, barely breaking to gasp before diving into another long kiss. She ran her hands over him, greedily taking her fill of his physique, not letting herself think about how to make this count. Rather, she steeped herself in the moment and savored every sensation, drinking in his heady scent, peppery and spicy, but musky and exciting at the same time. She bumped her thighs into his iron-hard ones, liking the sense he was undentable. Impervious.

Their tongues tangled and she groaned in sheer luxury, letting herself burn alive in the bonfire of desire building between them. His implacable strength seemed to overwhelm her for a moment, making her stumble, then she felt something against her bottom.

He lifted her, dress riding up at the same time, and sat her on the cold marble of the table by the door.

Before she could decide what she thought of that, he pushed her legs apart and stepped between them so they were eye to eye, mouth to mouth...

Kissing again. Deeply. Unreservedly.

The fine lace of her new Parisian panties snapped.

She gasped and closed her teeth on his bottom lip, waiting... *There.* He touched her, stroking lightly, just a tantalizing caress that made her flesh pulse for more. After a long, breathless moment he easily deepened his caress into her slippery folds.

Encouraging him with moans of pleasure, she inched forward and layered on openmouthed kisses, letting him know how good he was making her feel as he caressed her.

Velvety waves of pleasure rolled outward from his touch, making her limbs weak and tingly, her core tight and eager.

With clumsy fingers, she undid his shirt buttons, wanting to taste his skin.

He took his hands off her long enough to yank his shirt open, revealing his muscled chest. Natalie couldn't help but gasp and hook her heels against the backs of his thighs, urging him back into her space so she could splay her hands on him and take in all that burnished skin.

He resisted long enough to take something from his pocket, then he opened his pants. Despite how aroused and excited she was, a tiny niggle of nerves hit her as he revealed himself. They were doing this. Now. Here.

Jerking her gaze up from the condom he was applying to his very admirable erection, she looked into his face and saw a kind of blind passion that made her heart skip, as if a bucket of water had hit her, but it was hot enough to scald. He was as hungry as she was. Barely holding on to control. It was heady and exciting.

"Demitri," she managed weakly.

"You're incredible," he muttered, hooking one arm behind her to draw her to the edge of the table. Then his gaze caught hers and something like panic edged into his. "You're not with me?"

"No, I am. I want you. This. Now. Please."

His breath flowed over her lips as he released it in an expulsion of jagged humor and relief. Firm pressure nudged at her opening and she closed her eyes, not wanting him to see how desperate she was right now. Aching with need.

He pushed with inexorable power into her. A smarting sting took her by surprise, making her catch her breath and set a hand on his shoulder.

Rearing back slightly, he said, "You're not a virgin."

"No!" Her gasping laugh came out as a papery husk.

"It's just been a long time. Please don't stop. I really want this."

He made a noise between frustration and despair as he covered her mouth, kissing her with hungry desire, trying to persuade her body into softness.

She enfolded him with her limbs, drawing him in, making the penetration happen despite the discomfort so they were locked tight, both pulsing in expectation. *Yes.* She'd needed so badly to be held tight against a warm body, a man's hands caressing her as though she was treasure, his hardness filling her where she'd felt empty forever.

His head tipped back and he groaned at the ceiling. "You're killing me."

She smiled, easing her tight grip on him, but squeezing internally, signaling that she was ready. Needy. Scraping her nails against his sides, she bit his pecs, inciting him.

He drew in his breath as a fierce hiss, slitted eyes staring deeply into hers as he practically pulled her off the table and onto his firmly planted, hard body. Then he caged her with hard arms, one hand low enough on her tailbone to brace her on the edge of the table, the other hooked behind her knee, holding her open. From there it was primal, but so good. Basic he might be, but selfish he was not. Each thrust was possessive, controlled and deliberate. And he watched her the entire time, as though he was willing her to lose herself in their lovemaking.

She couldn't hang on to control, not when the crashes of their hips sent detonations of joy splashing through her. Feverish and acutely sensitive, she felt everything from the friction of her silk slip to the damp sheen on his hot skin. He ducked his head to set his teeth against her neck. She knew a love bite would be bad, but she arched to make it easier for him to mark her. She'd never felt so glorious, so sexy or desired or alive.

They made love with lusty groans and fevered gasps as

she greedily fought orgasm, loving the way he made her feel, filling her up and stroking his hand restlessly up her inner thigh, under her dress. Swearing gruffly against her cheek, he found her mouth with his own and her breast with his hand, pushing her bra cup up so he could pinch her nipple, seeming to shake with need as he quickened his pace and claimed her mouth as though she was his last meal.

"Now, Natalie," he broke away to demand. *"Now."*

His voice sent prickling sensations down her spine. The coiled sensation where he moved inside her deepened to a kind of tension she couldn't resist. This was good, but the other side would be better. When he thrust deep and held himself there, held her tight to him, nudging her through the door of ecstasy right along with him, she gave herself up to it, clinging as though they were falling from an airplane into the sky.

For a blind second it was that fathomless. Then the tumble of orgasm struck, near wrenching in its power. The release and contraction inside her redoubled as Demitri pulsed and rocked, his body arched against hers in ecstasy, his cries triumphant, extending her sensation so she could only gasp and tremble, utterly helpless to their combined climax. He held her so tightly she was sure she'd bruise, but she didn't care. Nothing hurt. All the dark spaces inside her glowed hotly. Her entire being flooded with bliss and perfection. She never wanted it to end.

But the quivering pulses eventually died away. Her awareness returned to their ragged breaths and the hard marble under her bottom and the coat of sweat on his skin against her own layer of perspiration.

Embarrassment struck like a hammer. She'd been so easy. She'd just had a one-night stand—literally with him on his feet.

Lifting his head, Demitri stole a few tissues from the

box near her hip and eased from her. When he stepped away and turned his back, she forced her weak legs together and prayed they'd hold her as she unsteadily found her feet.

He walked into the first door down the hall. A powder room, she imagined, but didn't stick around to find out.

Mortified, she grabbed her purse and left without a word.

Demitri was barely forming thoughts. Deep in the back of his mind he knew what had happened with Natalie was wrong, but that wasn't why he'd sought a moment to pull himself together. He was fairly shameless when it came to right and wrong, but not usually so audacious as to take a woman inside the door like a sailor with a doxy. He might get his date into the mood in the lounge, but he never lost control there, not so completely.

That loss of sense made him uneasy. He loved sex, loved the escape and pleasure a woman's body offered him, but what he'd just done with Natalie had been the wrong kind of mindlessness. As impulsive as he was accused of being, he typically knew exactly what he was doing at all times. How much damage and why.

In this case he'd cast any sense of consequence to the wind. She'd waved him in and he'd slid home.

And he wanted to do it again. In a bed this time. Again and again.

That was unsettling. He had a very healthy appetite for sex, but sex was sex and women were women. He never, ever thought things like, *I want her.*

Probably best to walk her back to her room and cut this short.

Avoiding his own gaze in the mirror, he closed his pants, but left his shirt open. One damp hand lifted to rub away

the itch of drying sweat on his chest as he walked back
to the lounge. His muscles still felt quivery and weak…

Where was she? Her coat was still there on the sofa,
so…

"Natalie?"

In the bedroom? A strange relief flicked through him.
The night wasn't over after all. He ought to be uncomfortable with her making assumptions, but all he could think
was that he could sate this disturbing desire to have her
again. How could he be this restless and hungry when he
was still buzzing with orgasm?

She wasn't in his room.

Of course, she wouldn't know which one was his.

"Natalie," he called, pushing open all the doors as he
went, even the ones to the room the children used, but she
wasn't in any of them. Kitchen?

As he went through the lounge, he glanced at the table
by the door and noted her purse was gone. A sick lurch
hit the pit of his stomach and panged a little higher when
he saw the scrap of black lace he'd snapped and discarded
on the floor.

Oddly uncomfortable with the evidence of their passion
lying where housekeeping could find it—*really* not like
him to have such a sudden and acute need for privacy—
he stuffed the lingerie in his pocket and glanced into the
hall outside the suite.

Empty.

Grabbing his room card, he went all the way to the elevator and hit the button. The doors opened immediately,
so the car hadn't moved since they'd left it less than thirty
minutes ago.

Baffled, he went back into his suite and did another
search.

Had she taken the stairs?

He dialed her room.

She answered with a brisk "Hello… *Bonjour.*"

"Natalie?"

A tiny pause, then, "Yes?"

"It's Demitri."

"I know. I recognize your voice."

Another pause, this one longer. He was waiting for her to explain why she'd left, but there was an expectant curiosity on her side, as though she was waiting for him to tell her why he'd called.

It dawned on him that she hadn't expected him to call.

When had he last called a woman in a timely fashion after a tryst, let alone within minutes of their parting?

"Oh, I forgot my coat!" she groaned in realization. "Rookie mistake. I'm sorry. That could be awkward, couldn't it? Can you sneak it into the small meeting room on the second floor first thing tomorrow morning? That's where we're doing the group training sessions. I'll pretend I brought it so I wouldn't have to go to my room before leaving for lunch."

"Sounds elaborate," he commented with false calm, feeling like the rookie here as a hot, spurned sensation followed the word *sneak*. He told himself to go along with her plan and count himself lucky she hadn't read more into their evening than was warranted, but he still found himself speaking in a low, uncomfortably dry voice. "I could bring it to you now. Or you could come back."

"People are going to talk enough after seeing me go to dinner with you. I'd rather pretend nothing else happened."

Ouch. He scowled across the empty lounge of his quiet suite.

"Is that why you left without saying good-night?" he asked. "You were afraid of being talked about?" Repercussions were not something he worried about. What she needed, he decided, was a demonstration of how quickly his credit card could swipe away any worries she might have. There really wasn't much that couldn't be resolved that way, and he was realizing that he'd happily pay whatever it took to get her back to his room and into his bed.

"I sure as heck didn't relish doing the walk of shame in the morning," she replied, delivering a second, startlingly efficient kick to his gut. Most women regarded sex with him as a badge of honor. Having her treat it as if it was something dirty was surprisingly demoralizing.

"I'm sorry if it was rude to leave like that, but it is a work night so I should, um, get some rest... I had a really nice time, though. Thanks." *Click.*

Seriously?

He set down the phone and stared at it, tension increasing by the second.

"Let it go," he said aloud, but his brain yelled, *Seriously*?

He looked at her coat draped over the back of the sofa. Defiance took him across to pick it up. Her scent wafted into his nostrils, confusing him with a swirl of misgivings and conscience and sexual hunger.

He put it down as though it was soaked in combustibles. His hands continued to tingle even when he closed them into fists.

She was doing him a favor, he told himself. They'd had no business taking a professional relationship to such a personal level. Leaving it as a one-night stand was absolutely the best thing to do.

Hell, the best thing *he* could do would be to put on a fresh shirt, go back to the club and pick up another woman. He would, he decided.

But didn't move.

In his head, he heard that movie star say, *I thought you were finished with her.*

The graveled anger returned to the pit of his gut and he didn't understand it. Yes, he picked up social climbers and took them to suites and nightclubs and lost them to celebrities. It was all part of catering to Makricosta's elite clientele. But Natalie wasn't part of that world.

The inconvenient integrity he'd shoved aside when she'd told him she wanted an affair returned with a twist of vengeance. Exploiting the innocent was one of the few things he tried not to do. The vulnerable were meant to be protected. His upbringing had taught him that much.

That was why he worked so hard to prove he wasn't innocent or vulnerable. He was jaded and impervious.

Why was he dwelling on any of it?

He crossed to the bar and poured himself a drink, scowling at Natalie's coat, thinking, *I'm finished with her.*

While her voice repeated in his head. *Walk of shame, walk of shame, walk of shame.*

Natalie was proud of herself for thinking to take the stairs last night. She'd run down them as though she'd been pursued, and had told herself she was shaking and breathless from the exercise, not as a reaction to intense lovemaking and a kind of shock.

That wasn't supposed to have happened!

Dinner, okay. That was fine. Going to the club had been ill-advised, but not terrible. A kiss good-night? Generally acceptable after a date, even if kissing that particular man was a bad idea.

Sex? She honestly hadn't planned that and couldn't believe she'd been so swept up that she'd gone through with it. In the front room!

At least anyone watching the elevator lights would have seen it stop at her floor then stop at the penthouse without any sign of it returning down to hers. And people *would* watch for little signals like that. As much as she loved her job and the people she worked with, she knew they were the usual assortment of society. Most were wonderful and generous, but some lived for gossip and drama.

Thank goodness a scarf was part of her uniform. It neatly covered the mark on her neck—something she really ought to feel more disgraced to be sporting, but she felt too physically good. Floaty and delicious, body aching in the best possible way.

Her heart ached in a different way. A rebound loneliness had struck overnight as she'd left euphoria and stepped back into reality. Her hookup with Demitri wasn't a forever thing. It wasn't even the beginning of a romance. She was just one more in his line of conquests. Tuesday night.

You used him, too. It's fine, she assured herself as she went about her morning. Her life had been one of constant responsibility and family obligation. Growing up, her brother's needs had always taken precedence over hers, and now Zoey's were the priority. Last night had been a rare chance for Natalie to completely indulge herself. It had been deeply satisfying in a poignant way. Not tawdry, as Demitri had intimated, but temporarily, out of necessity. She had a daughter and a life to go home to.

And men, she knew from experience, were just one more person with needs that wound up being put ahead of her own. If she had a selfish streak, it was in refusing to court deep involvements because she knew how easily she became a pushover once her heart was involved.

Even Demitri, who wanted nothing more from her than she'd got from him, had become someone she was going out of her way to protect. Not that she wanted to broadcast what she'd done with him. It was far too private. For a little while she'd let herself believe in the fairy tale, the one she kept closest to her heart and didn't reveal to anyone because it was so far-fetched. Other people got the dream ending, but not her. She knew that, but she'd been able to pretend for a little while that it was possible, and because that little glimpse of happily-ever-after would have to do her for a lifetime, she had no regrets that she'd taken the opportunity.

It left her emotions raw, though, and her heart in need of extra guarding. When her coworkers pried about the dinner, she insisted he was just being nice, and then pretended an annoying email had come through from her ex. After that, she was able to keep her focus on training.

Still, her colleagues watched her with avid curiosity as she went through her slides and explained the advantages of the new system. All the while, she was acutely aware of the empty chair near the door with her coat shouldered over its back. When they broke for lunch, one of the women who shared her office downstairs hung back.

"Is it true you had a date with Demitri Makricosta last night?" Monique asked in an excited hush of French.

Natalie blushed and shook her head insistently. "It wasn't a date. He bought me dinner, but it was a work thing. I'm doing a report for head office," she prevaricated.

"Oh? What kind of report?" Monique was friendly, but on the nosy side. The kind of person who needed to know things before everyone else. She'd pressed for all the details on the training before Natalie had got herself properly organized at her desk the first day.

"It's confidential," Natalie dismissed, letting her hair swing forward as she pretended to search her coat pockets. She had a hard time with simple fabrications like Santa Claus. Outright lies weren't easy for her.

"So Demitri didn't make a pass? Nothing suggestive at all? I find that hard to believe, given his reputation."

Well, *that* was certainly to the point.

"It's his voice," Natalie dismissed, smiling tightly as she applied lip balm she didn't need. "He doesn't mean everything he says to sound like a come-on, but it does."

"Does it?" a masculine tone asked behind her, making her whip around and ignite with heat. Not just because he'd caught her talking about him, but because he was a blast of supermale hotness. He hadn't shaved, his hair was finger combed, and his jeans clung like a second skin made of faded denim. Dark circles underlined his eyes, and his striped shirt was creased as though it had just come out of the package. He leaned against the door with smug corporate ownership despite his casually disheveled appearance.

That sexy tilt of his wide mouth was very self-satisfied, kicking her pulse into a gallop.

In a very deliberate way, he turned his attention to Monique. She blushed, too, standing a little taller, tummy sucked in and lips bitten flat with remorse.

"What do you think?" he asked Monique. "I only came here to ask Natalie to join me for lunch so we could talk more about that report she's writing, but do I sound inappropriate?"

He did. He totally did. Especially when he looked back at Natalie and she read sizzling memory in his eyes. His gaze stayed fixed to hers, but it felt as though she was naked and he was looking her over from nipples to knees.

Monique swallowed audibly.

"Lunch has been provided," Natalie managed, stowing her lip balm in her purse with hands that trembled. "Everyone's gone in down the hall, but I should join them. I promised to answer any questions they might have about my presentation."

She silently willed him to move so she could escape his aura of assertive sexuality.

"Theo sprang for lunch? He's usually such a cheapskate." Demitri stepped back from the doorway into the hall.

Monique giggled as she exited the room. Natalie was able to take one small breath before Demitri fell into step beside her.

Why was he here? It took everything to act casually as

the din of chatting people died off when they entered the banquet room.

"Good afternoon," Demitri greeted the crowd in French. "I'm stealing lunch. And Natalie. Fifteen minutes," he added when she turned a startled look on him. "In my office. We'll talk while we eat."

Unable to protest in front of their audience, she waited until they'd gone up a floor with their filled plates to the accounting offices above the conference level, passing a few curious pairs of eyes along the way.

The administration offices devoted to the siblings' workspace had a small executive lounge as its hub. Demitri walked her through it, then tagged his card on a reader before holding open the door with his name on it.

"What are you *doing*?" she asked as his office door clicked shut behind them. He was completely undermining the composure she'd worked so hard to put in place all morning.

He set his plate on the edge of his desk. She rattled hers onto the small circular table in the corner, but didn't pull out a chair. A surge of defensiveness accosted her, making her keep her distance and stay ready on her feet.

"I don't know," he grumbled, pushing his hands into his pockets as he confronted her with a hard stare. "I never sneak around. This is new territory for me."

What was that supposed to mean? She had reconciled herself to their thing being one night and him never talking to her again. His call last night had shocked her to her toes. This was even more baffling.

She had the sensation that her shoulders were up around her ears, locked with tension, but she couldn't make herself relax. Her heart was pounding, her body flushed hot and cold, her ears filled with a rushing sound… All of her was reacting to him in conflicting signals of excitement and danger while her brain hammered with the knowledge that last night shouldn't have happened. It had been self-delusional on an emotional level and just plain unprofessional.

"I don't…" She had to clear her throat, completely out of her depth here. "I don't know what you're saying."

He frowned. "Do you want it in French? I'm saying that I've never tried to hide the fact that I'm seeing a woman, and I don't like it. Don't expect me to be good at it."

"We're seeing each other?" Her ears rang with a repetition of the phrase, trying to make sense of it.

"Having an affair, then. Whatever you want to call it." He shrugged his big shoulders, the movement jerky and dismissive.

"Is that what *you* call it? I mean, do you even do that? See women more than once?"

"Not often," he allowed, not flinching from her bewildered stare, utterly unfazed at being called a philanderer. "But you said you wanted an affair while you were here, and last night was good." His eyes narrowed a fraction. "Very good. Wasn't it?"

Her heart seemed to break through the thin skin of her throat, pounding in a state of painful vulnerability under his challenge. His statement was nothing so insecure as a request for confirmation. He knew damned well he'd rocked her world, and given the intensity of his gaze, he was one feminine sigh of surrender from doing it again.

"Is there *any* chance you'll quit your job so we can do this in the open?" he asked gruffly.

"I… What? Ha!" The sound escaped her in a burst of disbelief as her consciousness landed firmly back on the hard floor.

She looked around, taking in weird details of his office that she couldn't have known if she was dreaming, like a slanted drafting table with a big scratch pad splashed with various streaks of color, a whiteboard scrawled with uneven boxes and illegible labels, a wall strung with threads, magazine clippings pinned along them. The shelves held dozens of odd items from water bottles to smartphone cases to beach balls, all wearing the Makricosta logo.

"Have I got this right? Are you seriously asking me to make a permanent change to my life for something temporary? That's not a demand for commitment," she rushed to add, holding up a forestalling hand. "I'm just saying, do you hear yourself?"

She almost added, *I'm a mom*, but it really didn't fit with the way she'd behaved last night and only made her more self-conscious with what was happening now. Especially because there was a small part of her that thought, *in another life…* She would never, ever wish away her daughter, but a wistful desire to see what might have been had underpinned all her very sound reasons for taking this assignment in France.

And here was the answer. This was what she could be: an independent woman who was carefree enough to take up a man's exceedingly frivolous offer of… What was he even suggesting?

"How would that even work?" she quizzed with bemusement. "I'd quit my job and you'd set me up somewhere, pay my bills?"

He barely moved, just offered a cool nod of assent. "You'd travel with me if I required it."

"Oh, my God." She'd been joking. Ridiculing the suggestion.

A gush of icy cheapness went through her as she absorbed the full impact of the scenario. This was what happened when you thought the grass was greener on the neighbor's lawn. Turned out it was actually an overflow of the septic tank.

She headed for the door.

Before she could turn the knob, his hand was over the

crack, his body looming next to hers in a radiation of heat and crackling male energy.

"Why does that offend you? I want to see you again and not on the sly. Whatever the obstacles are, I want to remove them."

She glared over her shoulder, trying to hang on to her insulted indignation, but he was so obviously uncomfortable it gave her pause. Her senses took a hit of his male energy at the same time, flooding her with memories of how yummy it had felt to be stroked and possessed and drawn into shared climax. Her breathing changed and so did his.

"Why?" she demanded. There were thousands of other women out there. He should know. He'd bedded most of them. Was he running out? Was that what motivated him to chase her?

"You know why. We didn't even make it to the bed, for God's sake."

Do not think he's calling you exceptional, Natalie. She had never been at the top of any kind of list, not even Most Reliable. She was straight-up, middle-of-the-road, work-hard-for-second-place stock.

But he was staring at her mouth like a kid at the penny-candy window, making her lips tingle and her insides twist in anticipation. She shook her head in disbelief, but he took it as refusal.

"Damn it, Natalie!" He shoved back from the door, crossing the room in a few steps, then swinging around to confront her. "Why the hell not?"

The feminist in her said, *I don't have to have a reason,* but she was so astonished by his reaction she could only speak the truth.

"Demitri, I don't *do* this. Forgive *me* for being lousy at *this*, but I don't go home with men. I thought…" She winced inwardly, not wanting to sound as though she was okay with a one-night stand. It made her sound as cheap as he was treating her. "I had this vision of getting away and being someone different, maybe having a fling since I haven't…" No. She would *not* admit it had been years. "Being away from home allowed me to behave in a way I wouldn't normally, but I can't continue doing it," she asserted. "Last night was just…"

What? An opportunity? An experiment? A much-needed climb back into the saddle of a horse she'd learned the hard way was expensive and ornery?

"It was a fantasy," she said, repeating what she'd told him last night. "One that shouldn't have played out, but I did it, and now I'm awake and it's time to be sensible."

Funny, Demitri thought. He'd spent the night coming to the realization that, for once, something real was happening to him. Being with her hadn't been an escape. It had been somewhere he wanted to go. That worried the hell out of him, but it had also pushed him to find her this morning and negotiate how they could continue seeing one another. And now he was remembering why women with standards were a pain in the butt.

"What's wrong with continuing the fantasy?" he demanded.

"You own the company I work for," she reminded.

A wash of relief went through him as he quickly dismissed that as an obstacle. "We've covered that. You work for my brother. And if you want to keep your job, fine. We'll work around it," he said, reluctant but resigned to that inconvenience. At least with that concern out of the way, he could give in to the pull between them and saunter into her space, brushing past her anxious "Demitri—" with a firm promise of "I'll show you a fantasy fling you won't forget."

"Don't." She pressed herself into the door, avoiding his

touch. "Please don't touch me. I have to face people when I leave here and—"

"You don't want to go back there obviously aroused?" he challenged, needing to hear it. To see it in the helpless flush and disconcerted cast of her gaze around the room before she brought it back to his, eyes deeply shadowed with painful desire.

He pressed his hand flat to the door beside her head, leaning close enough to smell the warm peach scent of her skin, aching for the graze of her rising breasts against his chest. Below his belt, a heavy rush of blood pulled him tight.

Flustered and anxious, she still managed to send a coy glance south. Her body arched ever so slightly so she brushed against him. She released a powerless whimper on a sobbing "Yes."

"I want you very badly, Natalie. Not after five o'clock. Now," he told her, willing her to fall in with his demands. To let him bend her over the desk and take both of them where they were screaming with agony to go.

Natalie heard the words and flinched inside, telling herself to remember who she was dealing with. She set her jaw and leveled her chin, forcing herself to stare into his black-coffee eyes. "Is saying that part of giving me the fantasy? Because I prefer honesty, Demitri. I'm pretty sure what you want is sex, not me."

He narrowed his eyes, displeased, but he only levered himself straight and said, "Do you know what vacuous means?"

Apparently it was a real question. He waited until she said, *"Yes,"* with an exasperated frown before he continued.

"Most of the women I've been with don't. And it shows. You're sexy as hell, but you're also interesting. Give me your number. I'll text you where to meet me tonight."

Just like that? Breeze right past *shouldn't* to *will*? Misgivings danced in her periphery, but there was no sick knot of guilty conscience that would have stopped her doing something truly immoral. Two unattached adults spending time together for a few nights was allowed, she rationalized. She'd be leaving on Saturday. Three nights out of her life to keep her warm for the next thirty years. It might make her cheap, but it would make her happy. She'd regret saying no.

When would she ever again have a chance to be with a man on her terms, without it impacting her daughter? This was the only time she could do something reckless and imprudent, selfish and deeply sexually satisfying.

With giddy excitement expanding in her chest, she heard herself giving him her number, saying, "You could have got that from my company profile. You realize that, don't you?"

"I told you, I'm not going to read about you when I can see you face-to-face and ask." His eyes came up from his smartphone, gaze warm with satisfaction and lit with anticipation. His carnal expression was exhilarating, but unnerving.

"You're really not going to read it?" she asked.

"Is there a reason I should?"

"No," she said with false calm. Three nights of sidestepping honesty and pretending she didn't have a daughter. That made her squirm internally, but she instinctively knew it would change everything, and she wanted the fantasy. She wanted to be a single woman alone in Paris having an affair with a hotel magnate.

And what an affair! They didn't come up for air until two in the morning, when she rose to dress, muscles aching, nipples abraded and loins tender. Oh, it was an amazing feeling. Her skin felt like velvet on the inside, luxurious and petted smooth.

"I don't like you going back alone at this time of night. Stay."

"I'm not going to walk. I'll take a cab," she said, even though it was only a few blocks. He'd booked this suite in a competitor's hotel for the rest of the week, he'd informed her when she had arrived to a candlelit dinner looking out on the Eiffel Tower.

They hadn't eaten any of it, consuming each other with a crazy appetite she put down to her years of abstinence and his years of building a healthy one. In her heart she knew this was bad, being such an easy conquest for him, but, dear Lord, he knew how to make it good for her.

"Bring a bag tomorrow," he ordered, following her into the lounge, casual in his nudity. "So you can go to work from here in the morning."

The man was incredible. Completely un-self-conscious, possessing more command unclothed than a decorated general. He was playful when he was relaxed, like right after sex, but he got straight to the point if things weren't going his way.

He was spoiled. Privileged and spoiled, yet so generous in bed *she* felt like the spoiled one.

He was dangerous, that was what he was. If she wasn't careful she'd start fantasizing about more than two more nights with him.

She crossed to the untouched table where the tea lights in their globe of water had gutted out. Stabbing an olive with a fork, she waved the little green orb at him.

"That's two meals you've made me miss—lunch this afternoon, now dinner. You'll be lucky if I don't go on strike for better conditions." She popped the olive into her mouth.

"Here I thought the package of benefits was enough to keep you satisfied."

Said package was twitching to life, making her grin right along with him. They locked gazes, and the prospect of returning to the bedroom crackled like a welcoming fire. But one of them had to show some control.

"Yeah, well, I guess I'm one of those high-maintenance women who can't be pleased."

"Ha! That is far from true, Natalie," he said in that husky tone he used when all his blood was rushing into one particularly prominent place.

"You're saying I'm easy?" Even though they were her own words, they went through her like a white-hot spear. She looked away from him, startled to feel the backs of her eyes sting. Why? Because she'd just remembered she was one in a legion of women for him? Because this was as good as it would ever get for her?

She dropped her fork with a clatter and headed for the door.

"Hey." He caught her up before she reached it, scowling when she stiffened with resistance against his hold. "What's wrong?"

"I just need some proper sleep," she dismissed. "I get emotional when I'm tired." And she was suddenly so homesick she could cry. She wanted desperately to hold Zoey. Right now. Her arms ached with need to feel the wiry strength of her girl. That was who she was: Zoey's mom. That was where she belonged, and she didn't need a man in her life, in any capacity, to make her life bigger or better.

She told herself.

He cupped her jaw and smoothed his thumb along her cheek. "Give me a minute to dress. I'll come with you."

"No, I'm fine." She couldn't let him become something she thought would fulfill her. She already had all she would ever need. Smiling flatly, she pressed the middle of his chest, tempted to let her touch linger on his taut skin, still able to taste his flavor on her lips, but she was her own person, apart from him. Had to be. "Good night."

CHAPTER FOUR

DEMITRI WAS TYPICALLY the one who needed space. That was how it had always been. Yet Natalie pushed him back a step and walked out.

Usually he created distance when the microcues of emotional discord began to manifest. He was deeply attuned to them, whether he wanted to be or not. His childhood had predisposed him to picking up the slightest shift in the air, when bad could go worse within the space of a heartbeat.

He'd learned to defuse those explosive situations with an outrageous comment or an injection of chaos. He stirred the soup very deliberately, taking control of the moment by drawing attention and forcing the detonation. The shrapnel never landed on him, so it had always worked for him to push the plunger or pull the pin.

This was different. Everything about Natalie was different. She wasn't clingy. She was defensive. Oddly quick to isolate herself even though she projected genuine warmth and affection. One second she'd been teasing, the next revealing a kind of desperation, but not looking to him to resolve it for her.

That was often the impetus for him to dust his hands of a relationship. The moment things grew complex and a woman grew needy, he slipped away. But Natalie hadn't looked to him for solace. She'd looked off into the distance, as though he was the last place she'd expect to find whatever it was she needed.

A bizarre, painful hollowness sank into him, urging him to follow her to the hotel and catch at the connection they'd had and lost without him understanding how or why.

Damn it, he didn't *do* introspection and angst. Especially over women.

Nevertheless, he found himself returning to the hotel first thing, snapping out arrangements that brought her into the hotel dining room with a harried look on her face. It was just before 8:00 a.m. Her hair swung in the sweep of gold he'd run his fingers through just hours before, and her warm brown eyes refused to meet his, instead taking a run around the table of three managers he'd assembled on the fly.

"I'm sorry. I just picked up the message about this breakfast meeting. I'm not prepared at all," she said.

"No problem, Natalie. It's informal. Adara asked me to check in on the software transition while I'm here, so I thought we'd have a quick round table over eggs and coffee." It was an outright lie, but he'd wanted to see her and figured she'd balk at something more private or intimate. This was an excuse to sit beside her, brush his sleeve against hers, memorize her lipstick print on her coffee cup. He resented every second of not having her to himself, but it was better than nothing.

She was the first to leave, anxious to get to her training session on time, she said, tilting her head over her phone as she left without looking back.

His mobile vibrated. He took his eyes off her and pulled out his phone to glance at the screen.

What was that? her text asked.

He grinned.

The first of three square meals, he thumbed into his keypad, inordinately pleased to flirt with her this way. I don't want you going on strike.

Who can I expect at lunch?

Who do you want?

Her reply took a few minutes, then, Just you.
He began to breathe again.

Meet me in our suite.

"I feel so Parisian," Natalie said as she put herself to-gether, one eye on the clock ticking toward the end of her lunch hour. She was pretending her attack of insecurity this morning hadn't happened, and he seemed to be going along. "Meeting a man in a hotel in the middle of the day is very French, don't you think?"

"I don't know. I've never done it."

"Met a man?" She laughed, pausing before applying her lip gloss to sit on the edge of the bed instead. "A woman, then."

He came up on an elbow, the sheet tangled around his hips, his physique seeming sculpted by an old master. His kiss was lazy and lingering, but he searched her eyes, mak-ing her drop her gaze.

"Are you embarrassed to be doing this, Natalie? Ash-amed?"

"No," she said, but even she heard the *not quite* tagged on to the end. The clock was ticking. No time to search out the words to explain how she was betraying a part of herself. "Are we meeting here tonight?"

"Would you rather go out?"

She shook her head, feeling foolish for her stricken neediness this morning when she'd wished for a moment that she was the only woman he'd ever known. When she'd wished she was the type to expect the best and had every right to receive it. When she'd wanted to be someone he found hard to please but longed to anyway.

It had been a silly moment of conditioned anxiety for a man to complete her when really she knew that was the real fantasy. Her father hadn't stuck around to help her mom. Her own husband had never really been there for her. If she sometimes yearned for someone to walk through life with her, to be there when Zoey was grown and spreading her own wings, well, maybe she'd look for that companion in twenty years.

Right now, this was enough. She had a gorgeous man showering attention on her, even if it was just physical. The here and now was pretty damned good. You had to embrace these things, even if they weren't perfect. That was what she'd learned from her brother. Merely having a good day was a gift. Take it and run.

And Demitri made her day *so* good. When he rolled her beneath him late that night, she was still trembling and damp with having taken her fill of him, but she was glad it wasn't over. He was still hard inside her, his body primed with tension.

"My turn," he said, closing his arms into a tight cage around her. "But that was insanely hot, watching you lose it like that on top of me. I don't have much control left. This might get rough."

"Okay," she said dreamily, hugging her quivering thighs to his hips, surrendering herself utterly to his control.

He groaned out a curse and clenched his hands on her shoulders. "Except I want to stay like this, so aroused I'm going to snap. What are you doing to me, Natalie?"

"Can't last to take me with you?" she teased.

A feral light came into his eyes, and when he moved, he wasn't rough, but he was deliberate and thorough, thrusting deep and driving her inexorably along the path he was taking. It was almost too intense to bear, but soon she was gasping, "Don't stop. Please, I'm so close."

"Now, damn it. Now."

He did get rough at that point, and she encouraged him, eyes open but vision white as they shattered together, crying out with jagged ecstasy while they turned over and over in the abyss of pulsing pleasure. The waves of joy went on forever, holding them in a paralysis of tense and clinging rapture, only fading enough for their hold on each other to relax, but they were still locked tight, his weight upon her, both of them weak, breaths uneven, hearts still pounding hard against the other's.

Dimly she grew aware that she wasn't going to get her breath back as long as he stayed on top of her, but she didn't care. He was sweaty and heavy, and her hip was cramping, but she didn't want to move.

"I'm a little bit afraid you're going to kill me, Demitri," she finally whispered, only half joking. This intensity between them put her utterly at his mercy.

He snorted and shifted half off her, sliding a lazy hand up to cradle her breast. "I've been thinking the same thing about you since that first night."

That made a funny bubble of optimism lift her heart, but she quickly ignored it. Turning her head, she kissed him once. More of a quick nip.

"Seriously. I *have* to eat. That croissant at lunch was not a meal," she complained.

He groaned as he rolled away from her. "You are *so* demanding. If you recall, I offered to take you out to dinner this evening, but you chose to jump my bones."

She had, and she didn't feel like dressing to go out now. They wore hotel robes on the sofa and ate picnic-style food he'd ordered this afternoon: cheese and bread, pickles and caviar, wine and strawberries.

Tell him, she thought, feeling close enough to risk it, but tested the waters first by asking, "You have two nephews, don't you? Do you spend much time with them?"

"And a niece." He paused, gaze drifting into the distance while a darkly introspective look came over his face. "But that's a long story. One I don't even know how to tell. And no. I have as little as possible to do with them."

Her heart dropped. "Really? You don't like kids?"

"I don't think they're a scourge on the planet that needs to be wiped out. But I don't…" He scowled again. "I honestly didn't think any of us wanted kids. I knew Adara was trying, but I thought she was just buckling to pressure from our father. He wanted an heir. I didn't think she genuinely wanted a baby. Realizing she did… And then Theo turning up with one. I was downright stunned. Worried even, because—"

He rubbed a hand down his face, stopping himself from continuing.

"Because?" she prompted, curious, especially when he revealed a flicker of conflict, something like remorse.

He shook it off. "Family skeletons. He's turned out to be a better father than I could have imagined, but it's been an adjustment for me. Suddenly I'm supposed to be this involved uncle and I have zero interest in the role. I will never be like them. Why? Are you dreaming of picket fences?"

There was a cool warning underlying his question that made her smile flatly. "I did at one time," she admitted. "But my father left my mom and my ex…" She sighed with all the dispirit he'd left her with.

"Did he hurt you?" His tone shifted to something that was both warmly protective and chillingly dangerous.

"No," she assured him. "Well, with his thoughtlessness. He's pretty self-involved, but he's actually…" A good dad. Not a great one. *Discipline* and *structure* weren't in his vocabulary, but Zoey knew without a shred of doubt that she was loved to bits, and that counted for a lot when love for his daughter had failed to keep Natalie's own father in the picture.

"My mother-in-law says we have to respect Heath's energy. That we're all on our own journey." She rolled her eyes, but then grinned with affection as she thought of Heath's mom. If she couldn't have her own mother, at least she had the best possible surrogate. If she'd had to leave Zoey solely in Heath's care for three weeks, she wouldn't have come, but Zoey's connection to her grandmother was special and deserved to be nurtured and reinforced. "He actually has a very nice family. I think that was what I was really marrying. His mother is a foster mom and takes in every stray orphan that happens by. I was in a pretty bad place, having just lost my brother when I started dating Heath. She was there for me after Mom died, too, so I can't hate him when he's the reason she's in my life."

"Very magnanimous."

"I try. But in answer to your question, no. Remarriage is not something I'm aspiring to." Especially with a man who had such low interest in children. "If you give someone the power to make you happy, you give them the power to make you unhappy. I don't want to be unhappy. So you're safe," she said, swallowing disappointment that she couldn't even talk about her daughter. She missed Zoey more and more each day.

Not that she'd be sidestepping that topic much longer. Tomorrow would be their last day—and night—together.

Except, unbelievably, it wasn't.

"What are you doing?" Demitri asked, emerging from his shower to find Natalie dressed in sweatpants and a slouched hoodie with a maple leaf on the front.

He'd left her sleeping since it was still two hours before she needed to start work, but he'd woken and checked email only to become annoyed at his brother questioning why he wasn't in Athens for a meeting. His first instinct had been to roll onto Natalie and forget about everything, but he was already making more demands of her than he had with any other woman, and that disturbed him. He'd hit the shower as much to prove his ability to resist her as anything else.

She didn't have the power to make him happy or unhappy, he kept telling himself, oddly unable to quit turning that remark over in his mind.

Now she was dressed and putting on her shoes, and his need to possess her climbed several notches.

"Being a master of disguise, I'll pretend I've gone for an early-morning walk to pick up some pastries," she explained. "Then it won't seem weird that I'm coming to work from up the block."

Impatience pushed out of him in an annoyed sigh. "This is ridiculous."

Surprised hurt flashed across her face before she schooled her expression. "It's only one more night."

A spike of ice nailed him in the chest. "What do you mean?"

"I leave for Lyon tomorrow. I thought I'd pack over lunch so I can come here right after work. I could check out properly and stay here my last night if you like, but that seems kind of—"

"What do you mean you're leaving tomorrow?"

"I'm catching the train. I did the same thing coming here, arrived on Saturday so I could get settled and see a few sights before starting work Monday."

"There's nothing to see in Lyon."

"Only two thousand years of history." She held his gaze, an unvoiced question in her quirked brows. *Are you asking me to stay?*

She didn't ask it and bent to tie her shoe instead, then

stood to shoulder her bag. "I won't bother checking out.
I'll just come over for—"

"What time are you off?"

"Might be as late as six."

"Do you ski?"

"That's random," she remarked. "I can, but not very
well. Why?"

"We can go to Switzerland for the weekend," he decided.

"Switzerland? That's crazy!"

"You're thinking like a colonial. It's not that far. I'll
take you to Lyon myself. On Sunday."

"But—"

She looked so fresh and innocent, face clean of makeup.
For a minute he wondered what the hell he was doing with
her. As cynical as she'd sounded about marriage last night,
the way she was hiding their relationship told him how uncomfortable she was with what they were doing.

"You don't want to?" he demanded gruffly, bracing
himself.

"No, I just didn't realize you wanted to..." She shrugged.
"I thought you'd have somewhere to be by now."

According to his brother, yes, but she wasn't talking
about work or any sort of external commitment. She was
inferring she thought he'd be tired of her. He should be,
and it made him uneasy that he wasn't.

On the other hand, a tension he hadn't quite acknowledged eased in him as he made plans to continue seeing
her. He was already looking forward to being open about
their relationship in Switzerland. This cloak-and-dagger
lurking in shadows was not his style at all.

Wait. Relationship? *Arrangement*, he mentally corrected.

She canted her head. "You're scowling. *Do* you have
somewhere to be?"

"No. I do what I want," he assured her. "And I want to take you to Switzerland."

"Do you?" she murmured, eyes dancing with laughter at him.

He scowled. "If you don't want to go, say so." And he'd commence with convincing her.

"I'll go. I just didn't expect this. Text me where to meet you when you've made the arrangements." She came across to lean into him, mouth lifted to press against his.

He took over the kiss. It had to last him all day, so he made it thorough.

"You can't buy me skis," Natalie protested.

"Why not?" he looked genuinely perplexed, even glanced down at his credit card as though he was checking to make sure it hadn't been declined.

"Because…" It was obvious, wasn't it? If he wanted to pay for a hotel room so they could sleep together, fine. And since he said his brother owned the helicopter that had flown them here, she supposed it was between the two of them to figure out how to pay for the fuel, but buying her ski equipment was weird. "What will I do with them after? I can't take them home."

"Of course you can. You ship to Canada, don't you?" he asked the clerk.

"Of course," the clerk assured her.

And the cost for *that*? Natalie drew in a slow breath. "I don't need skis at home, Demitri. I'll just rent a pair for the weekend."

"The line is too long."

"I don't mind standing in it. You do your thing and I'll do mine. We'll find each other on the slopes once I'm outfitted."

"*This* is my thing," he said with impatience.

"Getting your way is your thing?" she surmised.

"Exactly. Ignore her and outfit us both," he ordered the clerk.

"Demitri—"

"Come here. I want to show you something." He drew her over to the window, where snowflakes fell in glimmering sprinkles along the runs lit by high-powered lights. Against the indigo sky, the moonlight glinted off veins of ice in the jagged mountaintop. "Do you see that?" He pointed upward, to the ceiling.

"What?"

As she lifted her face, he kissed the daylights out of her. When he finally drew back, she blinked in shock, kind of embarrassed by their display, but also moved by the tender look in his eyes and the sweetness of his caress as he tucked her hair behind her ear.

"I just kissed you in public," he said. "We're here to be together."

"You could stand in line for rentals with me," she suggested with a cheeky grin.

"I do enjoy your sense of humor, Natalie." He reached past her and snagged a pair of lavender ski pants, the kind that clung unforgivably. "Try these on."

She glanced at the price, winced and said, "Okay, but I'm buying them."

"Again, completely hysterical. I invited you here. This is my treat."

Just going along with his demands didn't feel right, but what woman ever said no to Demitri? Before she knew it, she was decked out from head to toe, including goggles *and* sunglasses.

"It's night," she protested when he placed the shades on her nose.

"But the slopes will be bright tomorrow, even if it's overcast."

She gave up arguing with him, and they spent a couple

hours rediscovering their ski legs, left their equipment in a locker he rented and picked their way back through the pubs in the village to their hotel, eating fondue and drinking toddies while sampling live music. When they fell into bed, they were almost too tired to make love.

Almost, but not quite.

She fell asleep with her nose tucked into the damp warmth in the middle of his chest.

"You don't have to stick to the baby slopes for me," Natalie said as they leaped off the chair and snowplowed to a viewpoint. Far below, nestled in the valley, the village sat with comfortable old-world ease. Smoke puffed from small brick chimneys and snow-blanketed roofs poked up against sharp white peaks and brilliant blue sky. It looked like something off a Christmas card. "Go off and do some jumps or something. I'll be okay."

"The past two runs have been midlevel. I think you're ready to try something more challenging."

"No, they haven't," she denied, swinging her attention to him, then catching her breath at how urbane and good-looking he was.

His black bib-style ski pants over a white form-fitting insulated shirt, coupled with his sunglasses and natural air of command made him look like one of those intensely attractive villains from a British secret-agent film.

"I, um, don't ski well enough for midlevel." How had she even wound up here? The family hill she had skied during school trips at home had been a financial stretch. This place was practically coated in genuine silver, every piece of equipment sporting a designer label and mostly being used by licensed representatives, as far as she could tell.

"What are you talking about? You're cautious, but your skills are strong. I'm impressed."

He gave a passing nod of greeting to—good grief, was that a *royal*? Demitri had invited a gold-medalist and his wife to join them for lunch when they had bumped into them at the chalet, and a Swedish model had fawned over him in a gondola car. This mountain was a mecca for Europe's elite.

"Sorry about that," he murmured as an entourage in black followed the athletic frame of the prince down the slope. "I would have introduced you, but protocol says he takes the lead on that, and he's obviously preferring to be left alone right now. Ready?"

"Wait, no! Steep sounds scary," she said, catching at his sleeve and releasing a gurgle of nervous laughter, still taking in how he hobnobbed with the crustiest of the upper crust. "I'm cautious because it slants downhill. I'm used to ice. Flat." She lifted the hand not holding her poles and cut it straight across the air to demonstrate.

A snowboarder kicked off the ledge beside them and began to fishtail down the sharp incline, spraying powder back and forth with a *swish-swoosh*. Demitri had said he usually boarded, but he'd chosen to ski this weekend since that was her preference. She feared she was holding him back. He detoured for the occasional jump or slalom through a copse of trees, but kept returning to her side almost before she realized he'd disappeared, and always stopped with her if she needed a break.

"Ice? You mean skating?" he asked. "Do not tell me you played hockey."

"I'm Canadian. Of course I've played hockey. On a pond, not in a league, but I really meant ice dancing in a rink." She'd always thought the carving of skis into snow felt a lot like working skate blades against the ice, but speed gathered rather swiftly on a slope. She was so busy controlling that she wasn't paying attention to the signs, trusting Demitri to keep her from getting lost and keep her on the easy runs.

"Ice dancing," he repeated, taking in this new information with a bemused look. "How long did you do that?"

"Almost six years, I guess?" She wrinkled her nose. "Until Dad left and there wasn't really the time or money. I had a friend who drove me for a while, then I took the bus by myself, but Mom didn't like me sitting at the bus stop at five in the morning and…" She'd needed her. Gareth had. "It just didn't work."

"That's too bad."

"That's life," she said, shrugging it off. "It doesn't really bother me except, well, like today when we met your friend who medaled. I don't know if all the training in the world would have got me half that far, but he's just a guy who worked really hard. He made sacrifices, I know that, but it makes me think that if I'd been able to stick with my own training, I might have got a blue ribbon somewhere along the way. I really liked it and would have done the work. I wished I could have kept it up, but my life has never really allowed for the chasing of dreams."

He was looking at her as though he wanted to ask more, and she didn't want to talk about it or she'd get emotional.

"Okay, I'll try the top-level run," she told him decisively. "But if you get bored waiting for me to pick my way down, promise to go ahead. I'll meet you at the bottom."

"I'm never bored with you, Natalie," he admonished. "That's why you're here with me."

"Such a flatterer," she said, hoping he'd blame the tremor in her smile on the cold.

"It's the truth. But with the ice dancing, is it something you could take up again?"

"Gonna offer to be my sponsor? No," she said firmly. "It's not." She shifted her weight and moved in a comfortable glide so her skis were alongside his. Facing him, she leaned over, offering her mouth for a kiss. "But it's nice of you to encourage me."

"I'm not being nice. I'm telling you you're not too old. Seriously, what are the obstacles? The cost?"

If only he knew.

"You better take advantage of this now," she said with a touch of her gloved fingertip to her lips, not wanting to discuss any of her discarded aspirations. "In case I break a leg and have to spend the night in the hospital."

"I'm not going to let you break a leg. You know exactly where I want you tonight." He covered her lips with his own.

Demitri was in the kind of sleep he rarely found. Conditioned by his childhood to be a light sleeper—always on guard—he didn't often hit the really deep levels of REM, but he'd had an early morning, a lot of exercise, plenty of good food, a few glasses of wine in the hot tub and a delicious release with Natalie's humid gasps of pleasure against his ear. The room was cold, the bed warm, the smooth lobes of her bottom were spooned into his groin, and her breast was in his palm. He had found perfection.

Then a song like something off a kid's cartoon penetrated his consciousness. He fought acknowledging it, but Natalie shifted, coming up on an elbow to fumble for her phone on the night table.

"I'm sorry. Don't be mad," she said.

"Just make it stop," he growled, dragging her back into the hollow of his body, resealing the heat of her nude skin against his own.

"No, I mean I should have told you. Don't freak out."

What the hell was that supposed to mean? With his nose buried in her hair, he felt the tug of incomprehension pulling against the weight of falling back asleep.

"Hey, baby," he heard her say.

Baby? His mind sharpened.

"Hi, Mom," a little girl's voice said.

He snapped his eyes open.

CHAPTER FIVE

As Demitri left the bed behind her, Natalie tilted the screen on her phone so Zoey wouldn't see she had company. The fog of sleep was still befuddling her, but she was a mom, capable of pulling it together when her kid needed her in the middle of the night.

"Why are you up so late, sweetie? It's past your bedtime. Are you okay?" She'd talked to Zoey before leaving Paris, explaining she was going away for the weekend so might not be able to answer any calls. The fact her daughter wanted to connect anyway alarmed her.

"Daddy said I could stay up 'cause it's the weekend."

The door to the bathroom clicked firmly shut.

Natalie suppressed a wince and focused on her daughter. Zoey wasn't bathed, let alone in her jammies. "Where's Grandma?" She, at least, appreciated the value of a well-rested child.

"Auntie Suzie's baby is coming so she walked over to look after Bobby. She'll be back in the morning. Daddy said I could call you and tell you."

"Oh! Well, that is exciting news." They'd all known this might happen, so Natalie wasn't completely surprised. Heath was with Zoey and the worst that was going to happen was a late bedtime without a bath, but it still annoyed her that he saw no value in sticking to routine. "Babies usually take a long time to arrive, though, so you can't stay up and wait.

I want you to go to bed now, and I'll call you in the morning, okay?"

"But, Mom…" Always Mom lately. Never Mommy anymore. Five years old was way too young to make that transition.

"Listen, we'll compromise. You can skip your bath and have one tomorrow when Grandma is there to help you. Get yourself into your jammies and ask your dad to read stories, then you can play two or three games on the tablet if you want. You don't have to sleep, but I want you in bed." It was a trick. Zoey always dropped off like a rock once she was under the covers, especially after an active day on Heath's mother's farm.

Zoey agreed reluctantly. They said their "I love yous" and Natalie ended the call. Sitting up, she stared at the bathroom door, stomach as heavy as the pit of doom. Now what?

As the silence prolonged, the door opened. Demitri hesitated in the frame, naked and powerful, glancing at her with a chilling flatness that turned her to stone.

Her heart plummeted while varying levels of culpability, indignation and vulnerability washed over her. She should have told him, but he didn't have to act as though she'd committed a federal crime. As though he was not only furious, but wanted nothing to do with her now.

His view of her had changed, exactly as she'd feared. No matter how common single motherhood was these days, a stigma still existed. A judgment. Maybe she wasn't easy, but she was a woman who made bad choices where men were concerned. Someone who didn't have it together. A failure, and therefore her daughter didn't stand a chance. Natalie had been exposed to all those angles of prejudice at one time or another.

And she couldn't deny that she made bad choices where men were concerned, could she? Look at this one, giving her the silent treatment rather than asking her why she hadn't told him.

He moved to the chest of drawers and fished out a pair of shorts, stepping into them, and then continued to dress with efficient flicks of a collar and a snap of his jeans, all without looking at her. When he sat to put on his boots, she got the message.

"You don't have to go. I'll leave," she said, flipping back the covers and rising to search out her own clothes.

"It's fine. Stay." He stood and reached for his jacket off the hook on the wall.

She snorted, the furthest thing from amused. Angry, actually, that he didn't even want to talk about it.

Really bad choices, Natalie.

Wearing only her bra and underwear, she pulled her suitcase from under the bed, anxious to get away now. Feeling stupid and discriminated against. Feeling really, really hurt and disappointed, because yes, a very misguided part of her had thought he might like her enough that it wouldn't matter that she was a mother. It wasn't as if she was asking for marriage and a father for her child. Just a bit of companionship without being labeled or dismissed.

"What are you doing?" he asked, hand on the door latch.

She was obviously packing, but didn't see the point in being sarcastic about it. There was no reason to have a fight over this. She'd kept a secret and he was reacting exactly as she'd expected. Now they were done. It hurt, stung like hell actually, but there was nothing she could do to fix it, so she accepted it.

"Natalie," he said, demanding she respond.

"I'll get a room for the night, then make my own way to Lyon tomorrow," she said in as level a tone as she could manage. The nice people at her credit card company would be thrilled to extend her the cash. "You don't have to give up your room or your weekend."

"This was the last room. You're not walking down the street in the middle of the night with your luggage. *I'm* leaving. Stay here."

She turned, finding him with one hand still on the door latch, the other clenched so tightly around his dangling jacket his knuckles showed white. His face was all taut angles, his shoulders as stiff as iron, his will for her to do as he said practically resounding off him like rings of a bell.

"I want to leave," she said, not happy with the way her voice came out all papery and husky, but rejection did that to a person. She realized she was shivering and grabbed her long-sleeved undershirt off the floor to struggle into it. She found a pair of jeans in a drawer and shot her legs into them, then had to bounce on her feet to shake her butt into the seat of them. The rest of her clothes went from the drawer as an armload that got dumped into the suitcase.

"Natalie, stop." He was suddenly right beside her, tall and broad and reaching toward her.

She jerked away, pivoting to confront him. "I'm making this easy for you," she said with razor sharpness. "Stop making it hard for me."

"I have a right to be shocked," he said with a fling of his hand toward her phone. "Why the hell didn't you tell me?"

"Because I knew you'd act like this. Think differently of me," she blurted with a pointed, significant look. She couldn't hold his stare, though. Shame washed over her. All the guilt of denying her daughter weighed into her, slumping her shoulders so she skulked around him and into the bathroom to gather her things there.

Demitri listened to her clatter together all the millions of bottles and compacts and tubes she'd scattered across the tiny vanity since they'd arrived. His heart was pounding and a sick knot churned in his gut. Nausea had arrived with his realization that she had a child. Confusion and panic—yes, he was in a state of panic—had him desperate to walk out and pull himself together. Get away from whatever this was.

But she wouldn't be here when he was ready to come back.

That should be a relief. It should be exactly what he wanted because, damn it, that was how he coped best. Walk away. Pretend it hadn't happened. Leave the devastation for someone else to clean up. But *she* wanted to leave, and he was stuck to the floor, aware he didn't want her to go.

She wasn't the flirty, gamine, sometimes-nerdy single woman he'd thought he was maneuvering into a long-term position as his mistress. While he'd been delighting in finding a woman who had attained the perfect combination of being interesting while remaining disinterested in deep commitment, she'd been hiding that she actually carried the most indelible responsibility possible.

He was completely flummoxed as to how to proceed.

She came out of the bathroom and brushed by him without looking at him, almost as though she was too ashamed. *I knew you'd think differently of me.*

He was seeing her differently, but not in a bad light. It was more… Hell, he didn't want to examine any of what he was thinking or feeling. Face forward and keep moving was his motto. He never looked back and self-examined.

Scratching a hand through his hair, he watched her struggle to zip the poorly packed case and the word burst out of him. "Stop."

She only set her chin and worked to press and joggle the zipper tab with more determination.

"Natalie, would you give it a rest for a minute and just tell me—"

"What?" she demanded, quarter turning from the case and folding her arms, pure belligerence in her tone. "Tell you why I'm in Europe pretending to be a single woman who can have affairs?"

"You're not single?" That lit his fuse with a burn so deep and hot, he stopped breathing.

"No, I am. I'm single," she assured him with a widening of her eyes that told him she'd seen the switch inside him and was alarmed by it. "I meant about not mentioning Zoey. That I've been acting as if I don't have any obligations when I actually have a five-year-old." She pressed a hand to her forehead. "But I did tell you that first night that this is just a fantasy. A chance to live in a way I could never touch in my real life."

He told his muscles to relax as he watched self-consciousness flicker across her face. She met his eyes with a small plea for understanding in hers.

"I'm not proud of that. Or of hiding her from you. Heck, leaving her for three weeks with my mother-in-law has been eating me up, but that, at least, was for the sake of my career. It's actually what Gideon talked to me about that day you saw us."

She flicked another glance at him before she continued in a rush, as if she'd been dying to get this off her chest.

"Twice before this I couldn't take a special assignment because Zoey was too young for me to leave her. I was almost passed over for this one and wrote Adara an email about how it feels like discrimination when a married man with a child my daughter's age would be chosen without any hesitation, but I wasn't. She arranged for me to have this spot and asked for my input on rewriting the policies so they're more supportive to single-parent employees. They want to encourage everyone trying to advance in the company, especially if they're caregiving at home, because poverty doesn't help anyone in that situation."

Demitri nod-shrugged, vaguely aware of a discussion about that at board level, but it was so beyond his sphere of interest he'd let his siblings run with it. It wasn't the most impactful detail now.

"Your daughter is *five*? How old are you?" He'd guessed her to be twenty-five or six, but to have a daughter that old, she must have been a baby herself when she got pregnant.

She tucked her chin. "Twenty-four."

He couldn't help the way his brows lifted in shocked dismay.

"There was a party the night we all graduated high school." She shrugged. "My brother had just died and I was..." Her shoulder hitched defensively. "I'm not proud of that, either, but it happened and we got married because that's what you do, right? I wanted someone to take care of me, but Heath wasn't interested in taking care of either of us. He barely takes care of himself." She combed impatient fingers through her hair. "I shouldn't say it like that. I mean, he's not going to let Zoey play with matches or anything," she grumbled. "But he doesn't hold down a real job. 'Flash cards and dental appointments can be done another day, let's go fishing instead' is his attitude. He loves her and will always keep her safe, but I can't count on him when it comes to the day-to-day stuff."

The baleful darkness in her tone hit Demitri below the belt, bludgeoning him with the knowledge that he'd never been someone to count on, either.

"And this wasn't... I wasn't looking for someone to take care of me here," she rushed to add, indicating the room with a circle of her finger. "Skiing the Alps is nice, but I learned to live without any sort of frills a long time ago. I'm actually good with taking care of myself and Zoey. One of the reasons I don't date is because I don't want the hassle of trying to fit someone else's needs into our lives. We're solid, and even when I focus on my career it's really about her. Better income translates to more opportunities for her, a better education down the road. I'm trying really hard to make decisions that are best for her. But then

I had this little spell of time here to think about myself for a change."

She smiled with pained truth.

"You live single and carefree every day," she pointed out. "You probably don't realize how alluring the lifestyle is. Parenting and mortgage payments are not glamorous. And look at how you've reacted. You thought I was super-hot when you thought I was single and now you're turned off because I'm a mom. I wanted to *feel* hot and fun for a change."

"I'm not turned off," he growled, moving into the chair where he'd sat to put on his boots. His feet were heavy, his jacket on the floor where he'd dropped it.

He braced his elbows on his knees, deeply bothered and uncomfortable, still not keen to delve into why he was struggling with this, but he couldn't avoid dissecting it.

While she was already turning back to her suitcase to fiddle with the zipper, apparently resolved to leave.

"I don't mess around with moms, Natalie. I hear what you're saying," he hurried to state, forestalling another "you're a fantasy" remark. For some reason that was starting to annoy him. "The women I usually get involved with are as superficial as I am. You're not shallow in the least, and I knew that the first day we spoke, but I ignored it because…"

"Sex," she provided. "I know. That's why I'm here, too."

It was more than the sex. He liked her, but the sex was pretty incredible. Did she even realize how good? His conscience twinged as he processed that it sounded as though she'd had one lover before him, a boy-man who had never got past seeking his own pleasure.

A dark ache rose behind his breastbone. No wonder she was so enthralled with him. It had nothing to do with substance on his side or even his money. It was purely because he happened to take a great deal of pleasure in giving women pleasure, and she was starved of it.

He swore at the floor between his feet, oddly embittered by the thought.

She sighed. "I should have told you. I'm sorry. You're feeling guilty and you shouldn't. This was my decision, Demitri."

He lifted his head, grumbling, "Maybe your ex never gets a chance to take responsibility. Did you ever think of that, Natalie?"

She dropped her splayed hand from the middle of her chest, expression blanking with surprise. "Fine. Wallow in guilt, then. This is all your fault."

It wasn't, obviously, so he shouldn't be feeling anything beyond mild inconvenience that he was losing a delightfully compatible lover.

He rubbed his thighs, growing more keyed up as he watched her open her case and rearrange things, shoulders bowed with rejection.

Because she had a kid. And rather than try to pull him into that vortex, she was telling him why she never would. There was a quiet ferocity in her defensiveness. She was sorry she'd hidden her daughter, but everything she'd said told him she was deeply proud and committed to the girl. It was sweet and endearing, and he couldn't leave her thinking that he found something wrong with that.

"Nat, listen," he said to her back. "I'm allergic to family. Mine's a horror show. Like, we should be in therapy, but that would mean talking about it. If I could cut all my ties to them, I would."

"Don't say that!" She swung around. "If I didn't have Zoey, I'd be completely alone, and that's awful. Don't wish your family away. Don't."

"Obviously we have different perspectives," he dismissed, not comfortable with her vehemence. "What I'm saying is this does change things, but because of *my* history, not yours."

She hooted, swinging around to say, "It's not you, it's me? Is that what you're saying?" Heaving her suitcase off the bed, she let it hit the floor next to her with a thump that jostled her narrow body.

"Stop." He stood, hissing with impatience at her determination to leave.

"Look, I'm not going to tell the guy who paid for the room to get out of it," she stated. "I'm a big girl and can solve my own problems. I wasn't sleeping with you for this ski trip or even a new scarf." She pulled the silk one he'd bought her from its bunched home inside her coat sleeve and left it on the dresser. "I just wanted a nice memory. Let's keep it as one by ending things here, with civility. A clean break."

He had never realized how much that silly saying could feel like an actual bone snapping inside him, leaving a screaming agony that reverberated through his entire body.

"I brought you here," he said through his teeth. "Stay in this room, get some sleep and I'll take you to Lyon in the morning. Meet me in the lobby at eight. That's the end of it." In more ways than one.

He walked out.

CHAPTER SIX

DEMITRI HAD TWO limos waiting at the helipad when they arrived in Lyon. Aside from a few neutral remarks—*good morning, ready?*—they'd barely spoken. A maid had come to the room to pack his things. He'd piloted the helicopter and Natalie had tried to convince herself she was airsick, not lovesick.

They arrived at the Makricosta Heritage in Lyon one behind the other. He had no reason to check in and only a small duffel that he took straight to the elevators. She had new colleagues to meet and a room to be shown to. If she was distracted while she waited and her gaze followed the youngest Makricosta brother as he strode across the lobby, it was hardly suspicious. Every female employee's head was programmed to turn in his direction when he graced a hotel with his indifferent presence.

Her room, a standard queen in the upper middle of the main tower, had a pretty view of spires and red-tile roofs winding along the Rhone. Liable to break down if she moped in her room, really needing distraction from her melancholy thoughts, she asked to be shown to the desk she'd be using.

The administration floor was mostly deserted. The weekend manager pointed out her cubicle and leaned in with a conspirator's whisper. "I'd keep my head down and finish as quickly as possible, if I were you. The boss is in and does *not* look happy." He nodded toward the end of the hall.

"Demitri?" She willed herself not to blush. "I saw him arrive." And the idea of him looking as despondent as she felt should *not* be such a boon to her ego.

"Adara," he corrected under his breath. "But she's got him in there, and the staff in Paris said heads will be rolling, but they're being very tight-lipped about what happened. You were just there, weren't you? Do you know?"

She tightened her grip on her purse. What was left of her conscience swirled down an imaginary toilet. The dryness in the pit of her stomach affected her voice.

"No," she managed, but it was more a mouthed word than spoken. Her eyes had to be huge and swimming in guilt.

Fortunately, he was craning his neck as he ensured the doors were still firmly closed down there. "Well, I don't want to be around when they come out looking for blood. I'd suggest ignoring the rain and heading out to see the sights." He gave her a nod as he walked away.

Adara *knew*.

Natalie wished she could run and hide from this, but it was not her way. When she made a mistake, she owned it, 100 percent.

On heavy feet, she started down the hall.

Demitri so didn't need this. He reached for the knob on Adara's office door, only getting it open a crack before his sister said sharply, "We're not done talking about this!"

She stood behind her desk, more imperious than he'd ever seen her, but hard to take seriously when she had yogurt on her lapel. Apparently she'd been in a hurry to leave her family in Athens this morning so she could lie in wait for him and ruin the rest of what had already become a lousy weekend.

"It's over anyway, so there's nothing more to say," he told her.

"There's plenty to say! You've opened us to a sexual-harassment suit!"

"She's not going to sue," he said impatiently. Natalie was good and decent and maybe a little too grateful for his attention. They'd parted amicably—or as amicably as he could feel when he was furious with her for being completely different from what he wanted her to be. He would still be brooding over that if his sister hadn't arrived and *commanded* him to meet her in her office. *Now.*

She'd been taking lessons from her husband, he imagined. At one time Adara had been quite the pushover, determined to run the hotels but hiding behind Gideon and his position as chairman to do it.

The PA who'd nearly destroyed their marriage had turned out to be the best thing for them, however. Adara had grown a lot more confident once she knew her husband was completely devoted to her and always had her back. These days she really was the face and voice of Makricosta's, strong and determined.

Admirable, Demitri would have judged her, if she wasn't being such a pain in his hide.

"Everyone in Paris knows you've taken up with one of the IT specialists. It will be across the entire organization within the week. Are there others?" she demanded.

"No. And may I remind you that Theo did it? Why the hell are you coming down on *me*?" He could hear his voice tightening with anger at the injustice, and searched for patience. For the laconic disinterest he'd patented for any occasion when his morals were called into question. This was what he did. He behaved badly and it rarely had serious consequences. He rode out the waves he'd created and got on with his day.

Today his sister's castigation got under his skin. Maybe

because he was already so angry—he would still be with Natalie if not for her revelation, and company regulations could go to hell.

"I suggest you draft a new policy," he stated with a patronizing smile. "One that spells out exactly when it's appropriate to dally with employees. Because right now it appears to be a gray area."

"First of all, Theo offered me his resignation," she said testily, counting on a finger. "Even though, technically, Jaya was no longer working for us when they got together."

"About twenty minutes technical, from what I gather, but *okay*. I'll resign. Are you done?" Demitri said, dead serious, but she ignored his offer and touched a second finger.

"And he *married* her. Are you in love, Demitri?" she scoffed with cold disparagement. "Are you settling down to have a family?"

A hard fist clenched around his chest, suffocating his lungs and squeezing his heart so it pounded hard enough to hurt. No, he wasn't in love. What kind of emotion was that anyway? It was something that had kept their mother with a man who used her attachment to torture the bunch of them. Natalie was far too sweet and special to abuse with such a vile thing as *love*.

As for family, it was nothing but obligation and politics and bad memories swept under a rug. Did Adara not remember where they'd come from? Family was the reason he was the black-sheep clown that drew attention so it didn't land on her and Theo.

Resentment came up in a rush, gathering strength from her scorn. Did she think he had never wished he could be good like them? All those stupid, asinine, outrageous things he'd done over the years had been for *her*—trying to protect the two of them. If he had to spell it out for her, fine.

"You know what it was?" he challenged, lying, but

wanting her to see for once that he was loyal to the family in his own way. In the only way he could be. "I was keeping another opportunist from trying to poach your husband. I took one for the team, okay? If you want to fire me for that, go for it."

Adara went chalk white. He realized immediately that he'd screwed up, hitting her where she felt most vulnerable.

Remorse arrived like a westbound train, but before he had a chance to backtrack, the door he'd started to open pushed into him, knocking him into taking a step forward, clipping his shoulder hard enough to make him swear.

"What the hell—"

Natalie.

She confronted him with such horrified hurt that his guts turned to water. Her expression was shattered, her lips white and parted in disbelief, plunging him into a bath of emotion far worse than remorse. He wanted to slink away in utter disgrace.

"Really?" she demanded.

He opened his mouth, distantly aware of his sister taking in a shocked breath.

His brain rapid fired with reactions, all of them too revealing. Adara would realize how much Natalie had come to mean to him, and it was too much to let anyone see. Even Natalie, because she was shaking in a tremble of shock and rage, skimming him with a contemptuous gaze, as though filth coated him, filling her with repugnance.

He couldn't let her see how much that hurt.

"That's all it was?" she spat with loathing. "Even though I *told* you—"

"No," he protested, reaching for her arm.

Natalie knocked his hand away, adrenaline making her instincts fast and violent. She wanted to hit him. Punch and kick. She really did. Her heart was racing, her entire body hot, her ears ringing, her muscles twitching in aggression. She was sure that he'd believed her when she'd denied having planned to seduce Gideon.

"I told you I didn't expect anything except…" *A good memory.* So much for *that.*

She couldn't continue. Her face crumpled. Her control unraveled.

She shouldn't have walked down here thinking she could explain. She shouldn't have stood outside the door eavesdropping, hoping to hear he *did* love her.

Quite the opposite. He had complete disdain for her. He thought she was some kind of husband stealer and had only slept with her out of familial obligation. That put her somewhere lower than a pity—

She ducked her head, nausea climbing as reaction settled in.

She turned and left. Bolted from his call of her name and the equally sharp cut of Adara's voice. She dived into the first ladies' room she saw, eyes burning with tears she couldn't hold back.

She was such an *idiot.*

And now she'd lost her job. She was sure of it. They weren't going to fire *him.* The affair had been consensual. In its best light it looked as if she'd been trying to climb the corporate ladder. At its worst, Adara would believe her marriage had been threatened.

Fighting back tears, Natalie reached for a hand towel, but couldn't look herself in the eye to dab at her makeup. Her face ached with the effort of holding back a flood of emotion.

Men. Why hadn't she learned her lesson from her father, who'd left, and Heath, who hadn't really been there? Had she really expected Demitri to show up for anything but what she'd been putting out?

Heels clipped toward the door, and she swiftly stepped into a stall. The main door opened and Natalie heard a woman enter. The door whispered closed and a lock was turned. There was a sniff and a rustle while Natalie held her breath.

Through the crack in the door, she saw Adara dialing her mobile. She spied her own handbag sitting next to the sink. Damn it, why hadn't she grabbed it? This was a nightmare.

"It's me," Adara's tear-strained voice said.

Natalie opened her mouth, not sure what to say, but Adara continued.

"I should have told you why I had to come to Lyon. I think I just fired Demitri. Or he quit. I'm not sure." Another sniff, then an impassioned "No, it's not okay, Gideon! I feel awful."

Natalie let her head drop into her hand, wondering if this could possibly get worse. She didn't want to listen to this!

"Do you remember Natalie from the Canadian…? Yes? Demitri has been seeing her and— Oh, hell. I have to go. No, I'm fine," she added quickly, voice steadying. "But Natalie is in here. I can see your purse, Natalie," Adara said, making Natalie wince behind her hand and stay exactly where she was. Beyond the stall, Adara continued to her husband, "I'm fine, Gideon, honestly. Just upset. But I have to talk to Natalie. I'll call you back in a few minutes."

An expectant silence manifested.

Feeling cheap and pathetic, Natalie pulled the creaking door inward and exposed herself. "I swear to you I did not have designs on your husband. I would never, ever go after a married man."

Adara's mouth pinched. Her eyes were red and her makeup threatening to run, but she was still incredibly beautiful in her quiet and conservative way. Long dark hair, clear olive skin. She was class personified, and Natalie felt incredibly cheap being in the same room with her.

Adara pulled open a drawer and took out a makeup bag

along with a white facecloth. Her reflection smoothed to neutral, yet remained distantly defensive.

"Demitri said it to hurt me. He *wanted* to hurt me, which is why it did. He does a lot of infuriating things, but he doesn't usually set out to wound. Lately, though, everything he does seems to be an effort to push Theo and me away." She wet the facecloth and wrung it out. Her glance came up to meet Natalie's. "I didn't mean that the way it sounded. I'm upset." She held out the cloth to Natalie.

It seemed too nice a gesture, especially on the heels of such an insult. Adara was suggesting that if it hadn't been Natalie, Demitri would have taken up with a different employee just to alienate his siblings.

She really didn't want to think he was that childish or that mean.

She'd like to think Adara was only saying it to spite her, because she was angry, but Adara wasn't angry. She was watching Natalie with a pleading gaze, her expression so sympathetic it could only mean she pitied Natalie for becoming a weapon in a family feud.

Natalie came forward to accept the cloth, more to hide her face than dab at her ruined makeup. Adara pulled a second from the drawer and worked on her own, making Natalie feel even more foolish as they repaired themselves in thick silence.

"I don't…" Adara began, then tsked as her phone chimed with a request to connect. "Not yet, Gideon," she muttered, adding with a sober look toward Natalie, "He worries. Especially when it's family stuff."

After a brief bit of typing, which Natalie assumed was a text to her husband, Adara set down her phone and gave Natalie an apologetic look. "My business head is telling me to record this and say as little as possible, but I can't do that. Natalie, I'm sorry."

"For what?" Natalie asked, askance. "I knew what I was getting into."

"I highly doubt that." Adara offered a tight smile.

Natalie had to look away. Adara was right. She had thought that at the very least their fling was based on mutual attraction and desire. Instead... Humiliation ached through her and would for a long while.

"I can't protect all of womankind from my brother," Adara said gently, as if she knew what Natalie was suffering. "If he wants to pick up good-time girls looking for a night of partying, I can't stop him, but employees are off-limits. He knows that."

"*I* know it," Natalie insisted.

She was being punished for self-indulgence. It wasn't that she wasn't allowed to be happy. She just had to be happy with less than what most people got. She'd figured that out a long time ago. Wishing for things that other people took for granted, such as having a dad or a healthy brother or a functioning life partner was futile. But if she kept her expectations low, she could usually have that much.

If she hadn't stood outside that stupid door, yearning for love and marriage, she could have *had* the poignant memory she'd wanted from Demitri in the first place.

Adara dug an eyeliner from her bag, then leaned into the mirror to draw fresh lines around her lids.

Natalie opened her own purse and searched out a lipstick, but she really didn't see the point in fixing makeup she'd cry off as soon as she reached her room.

"It's not as if I expected anything to come of this. I just wanted..." Her mouth struggled to form words. Her hand was trembling, her whole body still reacting while her mind tried to latch on to logistics so she wouldn't melt into a complete mess. Dread and guilt mixed with regret and embarrassment. "Getting involved with him was my decision. My mistake. I just…" Time to grovel. And keep her expectations realistic—she hoped. "Will you let me put in a resignation rather than leaving me with a termination on my record?"

"I'm not firing you!" Adara lowered her hand and straightened to face her. "Don't be ridiculous. And you're not quitting, either. If you need some time, I'll arrange for you to go home early—and believe me, I'll understand. Take paid leave while the gossip dies down if you need to, but I can't imagine who we could possibly find to replace you. We'll have to make a statement of some kind, too. I'm sorry about that. Your privacy will be protected as much as I can manage, but as a company we can't be seen as trying to cover up, especially because he's family. Legal will have to walk us through exactly how that part should be handled."

"I didn't mean any of this to happen," Natalie blurted, feeling the press of tears rise to brim her eyes. "I'm so sorry."

"This is Demitri's disaster, not yours," Adara scolded. "I'm upset it happened, but not entirely surprised. I wish he would—" She pressed her lips flat and seemed to deliberately force her despondent expression into something more stoic. "I won't bore you with our family issues. But tell me, would you prefer to go home for the week or soldier on?"

Natalie desperately wanted to go home and lick her wounds, cuddle her daughter and let maternal love heal the cracks that romantic longings had fissured through her heart. But the fact that she still had a job was a miracle in itself. No way could she walk away from it and jeopardize it further.

"If you really want me to, I'll stay."

Demitri was drunk. Not stinking drunk, but drunk enough not to care how unhappy he was. It was the perfect state to be in as he sat beside the pool of a competitor's five-star hotel in the south of France. No chance of sitting beside one of his own—his brother had canceled all his key passes along with his company credit cards.

That was after his brother-in-law, Gideon, the *real* head of the Makricosta organization, had had him escorted off the Lyon property. There'd been a phone call first. He had to give Gideon credit for wanting his side of things, but Demitri had been in no state of mind to be civil. "Adara's not sure if she's fired you or you've quit," Gideon had said.

Demitri had told him what he could do with his job, so furious by the way things had gone, he'd cut all ties to Gideon, his siblings and the damned hotel chain.

Do you love her? he could still hear Adara saying. *Are you going to marry her?*

It was supposed to have been a simple affair, not something that would haunt him. Not something worth quitting his job over.

He didn't care about his job. Not really. Certainly not about the money. He had a trust fund he rarely touched. He'd only gone into the family business for them. Adara was the one who cared about the hotels. Theo, well, Demitri would never understand why Theo was still there. At least he, Demitri, *liked* the kind of work he did. He was competitive enough to make sure all his campaigns and strategies were exceptional, even if he was bored out of his skull with the subject matter. Aside from Theo getting on his case about budgets now and again, neither of them had reason to question the quality of his work. They were going to miss him long before he'd miss them.

Which was proved when he saw Theo scanning the crowd from across the pool.

Demitri let a smirk of satisfaction tilt his mouth. He had known they'd break first. Come begging.

Theo spotted him and a twitch of disgust tightened his mouth.

Oh, goodie. A meaty, overcooked lecture, coming right up.

He watched Theo wind his way through the occupied deck chairs and families around tables. Theo paused at one, speaking to a mother with a baby on her lap.

Missing his own baby so much he had to stop and tickle the chin of a stranger's? God, he was sick of how besotted they all were with their spouses and babies.

Theo handed over a business card to the man at the table, hands were shaken and the baby gathered up by Theo. He walked purposely toward Demitri, the baby beginning to reach back and cry as he realized he was being taken from his mother.

"Is Makricosta's starting a black market—?" Demitri began.

Theo plopped the bawling kid into his lap, making Demitri scramble to set aside his vodka tonic and hang on to the squirming boy so the tyke wouldn't pitch himself onto the marble pool deck.

"What the hell?" he said to Theo, raising his voice to be heard over the growing volume of the worked-up kid's bellow.

"Make him stop," Theo challenged.

Demitri would have risen and carried the brat back to his mother, but was a little too drunk to trust himself, especially when just keeping the boy in his lap was like wrangling a marlin.

"Make your point, Theo," he demanded.

"It's pretty distressing, isn't it? Is he hungry? Does he need a diaper change?"

"He wants his mother," Demitri said pointedly. "Take him to her."

"What if his mother is passed out from drinking and

pills?" Theo said, leaning a hand on the arm of Demitri's chair as he mentioned the unmentionable. "What if you're a little girl and if you don't keep him quiet, your father is going to backhand you so hard you hit the wall on the other side of the room?"

"We're doing this here? Now?" Demitri asked, reminding himself not to crush an innocent baby just because his brother made him see red. Did Theo think he didn't remember? That he wouldn't have stopped their father if he could have? That he hadn't tried in the only way open to him?

"I'm sorry," a woman said, pushing in to break the men's intense eye contact. It was the boy's mother. "I can't bear hearing him—"

"It's fine. Perfect," Theo said, straightening into his hotel-controller role. "I appreciate your loaning him to me. As I said, just call my personal number when you've decided where you'd like to stay. Two weeks, any Makri-costa resort. Room and meals on me. Thanks."

"That's awfully generous for such a penny-pinching bastard," Demitri said as the woman walked away and the baby quieted.

Theo ignored that and only said, "Adara is worried about you."

"Really? Weird, because she sounded more worried about the reputation of the hotels when we last talked."

"She doesn't deserve the silent treatment. Text her and let her know you're alive."

"Take a look, Theo," Demitri said with a wave at his mostly naked, semireclined form on the lounger. "I'm a grown man. Why don't you two stick to playing mommy and daddy with your actual children?"

"Why do you always have to make things harder, not easier?" Theo muttered, crossing his arms and shaking his head with disgust.

It might as well have been one of those backhands Theo had been talking about, only for once, it had landed on him. *You have to be good, Demitri.* Yet being bad had been the only way he'd known to defuse their father's lashing out.

The guilt that had always sat in Demitri for getting away with so much, setting him apart from his siblings, slithered in him like a venomous snake, sinking fangs behind his heart. He'd always known in the darkest corners of his soul that Theo must blame him. Must secretly hate him. That was why he hadn't asked all the questions he had about Nic, fearing the answer would be, *because you're not one of us.*

"What do you want from me, Theo?" He wasn't going to beg for their acceptance. Adara had made it pretty clear what she thought of his ability to contribute to family. Did their tolerance of him hinge on his doing as he was told? "Do you want me to toddle on back to my room? You know he's dead, right? You're not going to get belted this time if I stay here and do whatever the hell I want."

It was too far. He saw the same look come over Theo that Adara had worn when he'd made his brash claim that Natalie had been trying to move in on Gideon. He hadn't been aiming for Theo's internal organs, but that was where his sarcasm had landed.

"Damn it, Theo," he said tiredly. "You started it—"

"No. You're right." Theo blinked once and revealed a gaze that was so devoid of emotion, Demitri knew he'd been wiped from his brother's short list of people he'd die for. "You do whatever the hell you want. Sit here and drink like him and act like him and don't give a damn about anyone else. We're better off without you if that's your attitude. I'll let Adara know she's wasting her time being concerned. I look forward to not receiving your calls."

"You look like a waiter," Demitri wanted to call at Theo's white shirt and black pants as his brother retreated.

He didn't trust his voice, though. When he reached for his glass, his hand shook and the taste of it made his gut churn hard enough he thought he might throw up.

If they had just left him alone about Natalie...

But he knew who had really caused this chaos. They all thought they knew about protection, but for years he'd done everything he could to keep his sister from getting knocked around and his brother from being beaten.

They didn't need his high jinks anymore, though. They were settled and happy with their little families. He only had a place among them on their terms.

He hadn't felt alone with Natalie. Not that he'd ever considered himself reliant on anyone. Until her, he'd *always* felt one step removed. Different from his siblings, not like other people.

But he'd *had* Adara and Theo. He'd always had their back, and he'd always wondered what it would take for them to turn theirs on him. It had been his secret fear: losing them.

Which was why their picket-fence marriages grated. He could trace all the twists and turns starting pretty much from when their father had died and Adara had looked up Nic, bringing him into their lives as if he had a place there. But those were just steps that had led to this moment, when his siblings not only didn't need him anymore, they didn't want him.

Natalie had wanted him. Not the way that other women did. Not because of his money. Maybe because of his proficiency in bed, but also because he'd made her laugh.

She'd made him laugh. She'd been a bit of a feminist, quite a history buff, quick to weigh in on current affairs. She'd been thoughtful and sensitive, and he'd wanted more time with her.

God, he hated himself for hurting her.

Pushing his thumb and forefinger into the corners of his

eyes, he tried to quell the pressure there, wishing futilely for someone to sort out this mess he'd made.

No one was going to show up this time, though. He was exactly where he'd always feared he'd wind up.

Completely alone.

CHAPTER SEVEN

AFTER LEAVING LYON, Natalie had managed to avoid going into any of the hotels for more than a month, thanks to a snowstorm that had turned the company Christmas party into a bust.

The whispers and stares had been pretty bad by the time she'd left France, but she'd taken it on the chin and powered through her assignment. Adara had defused some of the gossip by making a statement that Natalie's special contribution working with high-level management would ensure all employees, regardless of obligations at home, would be given the same opportunities in future.

This, along with a statement that Demitri had left the company to pursue his own interests, had all become old news by the time Natalie was required to show up for the quarterly departmental meeting at the Montreal location.

The meetings were as predictable as clockwork, always taking place on the second Wednesday of the first month. They always had morning one-on-ones with various departmental managers, then a catered lunch followed by a presentation of slides and reports. Theo called in his contribution by webcam, taking questions before turning the afternoon over to the Canadian IT manager, who always closed with breakout brainstorming sessions based on the morning's findings.

Each of these teams was making their presentations

when Natalie was handed a message by a bellman who'd slipped in to find her.

Your car will be waiting at the main entrance at four-fifteen.

What car? She didn't get a chance to ask and had to make her way to the front of the hotel when the last presentation finally finished. The limousine windows were blacked out and the chauffeur forestalled the bellman to open the back door himself.

Natalie caught sight of male legs on the far side wearing black jeans and motorcycle boots. She bent to see Demitri glance up from his tablet. The collar of his sharp peacoat was turned up against his scruff of stubble, making him look as rakish and devil-may-care as he truly was. His hair, needing a cut, looked ruffled by fingers, making her think of all the times she'd done it with her own.

Her heart rose to throb painfully in her throat, leaving a hollow feeling in her chest that threatened to cave in upon itself. She strangled out, "No." Then she straightened to force a smile for the chauffeur, repeating a tight, "No."

It was the only word she could manage. Her limbs began to tremble.

"Get in the car, Natalie. Or I will get out," Demitri threatened, voice so low she barely heard it, but so implacable she had to take heed.

Alarm, the kind that accosted with sharp tingles down her arms and legs, had her looking around at the curious doormen and her IT colleagues who were leaving the hotel for the transit stations, glancing at her as she stood next to the open door of the limo. She could hear their thoughts, wondering how she afforded a private car.

She did *not* need to stir up gossip again.

Ducking to speak to Demitri, she claimed, "I have my own car."

"You take the bus into the city in the winter so you can read, rather than having to pay attention to road conditions." He tossed his tablet onto the seat opposite. "You told me. Want me to get out and reminisce about the other things you shared with me?"

She narrowed her eyes into lethal death rays at him.

He reached for the door latch and gathered himself.

"I have places to be," she told him, making him pause and look at her. "A *daughter* to collect and make dinner for."

If that had any impact on him, it didn't show on his impervious expression. He only stated, "I'll take you wherever you want to go. But I want to talk."

About what?

She didn't suppose she'd find out unless she climbed into the car.

A sharp wind was cutting through the breezeway, pulling at her hair and the open lapels of her coat.

With an annoyed huff, she swung her laptop bag on to the seat next to him, then plopped herself into the seat opposite so she was diagonal to him, about as far away as the confines of the car would allow. Warm, at least, if not happy.

She gave the chauffeur her address and he closed the door. The privacy window was already up, and seconds later, the car pulled onto the road.

Natalie folded her arms and stared sulkily out the side window. "Someone told me once that only lowlifes pick up women at the sidewalk. He would know, I suppose."

A pause in which she refused to look at him. He was probably laughing at her. At the sort of treatment she accepted from men.

"You look good, Natalie," he finally said.

She snorted, because she'd been feeling wan before

she'd even made the trek into the city this morning. Zoey had been sick earlier this week, was finally well enough to be back at school, but Natalie was still shortchanged on sleep, always too worried when her daughter ran a fever to rest properly, and sitting backward in the car was making her ill.

Without explaining, she shifted to the other seat and snugged her coat collar up around her throat, returning her disgruntled scowl to the window. It had snowed while she'd been inside all day, just enough to drape the city in a fresh layer of white. Just enough to snarl traffic and persuade more people than usual to use transit rather than drive. The commute would have been a killer. She was secretly thrilled to have door-to-door service.

"I was angry with my sister and looking for the quickest way to shut her up," Demitri said quietly beside her. "That's the only reason I suggested you were going after Gideon. I didn't mean it."

If that was supposed to be an apology, he'd missed the most important word.

"She could have fired me." Her voice cracked, more from hurt than anger, but she hoped he didn't realize that. "I need my job, Demitri. I have a mortgage and a child to feed." Did he think she hadn't spent countless nights having this conversation in her head, where she railed at him and told him what a jerk he was?

Yet, when he sat beside her smelling all masculine and foreign with his special European blend of aftershave and a take-away espresso in the holder beside him, she couldn't help remembering how those scents had surrounded her in bed, clinging to the sheets and her skin. Making her close her eyes in dreamy memory of physical satiation.

"I'm lucky she didn't take you seriously," she muttered, scoring herself with the memory of that day even though it was something she had spent a lot of time actively forgetting. "But your real motivation is just as awful, so *whatever*, Demitri."

"What do you mean?" he asked in a dangerous tone that almost made her look, but she kept her head stubbornly turned away.

"Adara told me how you were looking for ways to dig at her and Theo." She worked hard to keep her tone flippant, trying to act as if this was merely something annoying rather than devastating. "That you probably would have slept with any employee just to tick them off." It made her raw inside to say it. She was insulted and sad. Very, very hurt.

"She said that?" His voice hardened with ire, stilling the swirling ache in her heart. "Look at me," he commanded, making her turn her head with a reflexive jerk. Outrage pulled at his expression. "She said that to you," he confirmed, looking straight into her eyes with aggressive demand. He was incensed.

Which was disconcerting. A little alarming and even heartening, since he seemed so insulted, but she reminded herself he was no choirboy. He passed along his dates to rock stars, among others.

Mentally willing her pulse to settle, she lifted her chin, trying to appear as unaffected as she wanted to be.

"Are you saying she was wrong?" She tried to sound bored, and hated that silken threads of optimism wound through her. And she braced herself for hard truth if he allowed that, no, Adara hadn't been wrong. Natalie had been trying to reconcile herself to that reality for weeks, and it still shredded her insides. "You weren't using me?"

"No. I wasn't." His gaze flinched away from hers as he looked forward. "Maybe I can see why she'd think so, but to say something like that… That's offside, Nat. I'm really angry with her for that."

She sputtered a laugh of disbelief. "Why? You said something awful and so did she."

"I didn't say it to your face. I didn't *mean* it," he shot back, dark fire brimming in his eyes as he looked at her again.

His fury was a stab into an abscess. Revisiting that day hurt so much she could barely stand it, yet his anger on her behalf released a painful pressure she'd been trying to get used to since it didn't seem as if it would ever go away.

That bleeding of acute pain edged her dangerously close to forgiving him, though. To thinking everything that had transpired had been okay. It hadn't been.

"Adara wasn't trying to hurt me," she muttered. "She was a lot nicer to me than I deserved, considering what I'd done. What *we* did." She drew in a long breath that burned. "We never should have…" She flicked her free hand at the interior of the limo, "This shouldn't be happening, either. There's no point. Why are you even here?"

Demitri studied Natalie's face, not liking to see her so unhappy, mouth pulling down at the corners as she looked away again. He'd been starting to think she wouldn't show, trying to find her home address on his tablet, when the door had opened and he'd heard her voice calling goodbye to a colleague.

The brooding disinterest that had weighed on him for weeks had lifted like clouds revealing the sun. His blood had burst with a zing of enervation in his veins and his nostrils had sharpened in search of her scent. For a moment he'd seen only her torso and legs, uniform eschewed for a chic pair of knee-high boots, tights, a tweed skirt and a cashmere top, all glimpsed from the open flaps of her long red woolen coat. Lissome thighs. Round, deliciously weighty breasts that he loved to cup and fondle.

Then she'd bent down to look into the car, and her curious frown had flattened to shock followed by complete rejection. *No.*

Not something he'd heard often in his life.

And now, *there's no point*.

He sighed, not having entirely thought this through. He'd simply realized a few days ago that given Theo's precision schedule for his communication meetings, there was an excellent chance Natalie would be in the Montreal conference rooms today. He was doing a lousy job forgetting about her, and he'd never been one to sit back and ponder when he could be taking action, so…

"Knowing what you thought—well, what I thought you thought—about my reasons for sleeping with you, made me feel…" The unbearable churn of guilt and shame returned full force to grind within his chest. "It made me feel. Period. I don't normally have a conscience or listen to it, but hurting you has been sitting on mine."

He let her see his regret.

Her mouth quivered briefly before she pressed her lips flat and looked away.

"Apology accepted, as thin as it is," she said stiffly.

"I rarely apologize. I can't be expected to be good at it," he retorted, stung. This conversation was not alleviating his inner turmoil at all.

"Sorry," she grumbled, smoothing an eyebrow, then glancing at him, somber and sincere. "I don't like conflict or bad feelings. I mean it. Apology accepted. You didn't mean for me to overhear you, didn't mean what you said. Adara had it wrong. Whatever we had was just…whatever it was."

"It was good, Natalie," he told her, reaching across to cover the hand she dropped to the seat between them. "You know that."

So good he hadn't been with another woman since. Which was driving him insane. He was *not* used to going without sex, and every woman he took out, trying to forget Natalie, was such a poor imitation he couldn't bring himself to do so much as kiss them. He'd come here thinking there must be a way...

Her eyes widened as if she was reading his thoughts. She snatched back her hand.

"Oh, no," she said firmly. "The position of man-child is already taken in my life, Demitri."

Perhaps the blow wasn't undeserved, but it was brutally placed on an open wound Theo had kicked through his psyche. Given the breadth of responsibility he *felt* like he'd carried all his life, he was stung by how little she thought of him.

"That was cruel," he told her, not entirely successful at affecting a casual tone.

"Did you honestly think we could just pick up where we left off? Are you forgetting I have a daughter? She's the reason you broke things off in the first place."

He clenched his teeth. There was a very convenient emotion called denial that had allowed him to set her daughter on a shelf while he had traveled here from New York. It wasn't that he wanted to pretend the girl didn't exist. But every time he tried to imagine how the edges of his life might accept the invasion of her daughter's, he recalled Adara's disparagement of his ability to be a family man. If his own sister couldn't see it in him...

Then Theo's "act like him" comment would echo in his head.

That one still burned. He would never, ever hurt a child, and that wasn't really what Theo had been suggesting. No, he'd been tarring Demitri with the man's selfishness and bent values of pride and superiority over empathy and caring.

The vilification kept rubbing at Demitri's rawest edges because he couldn't refute it. He didn't know if he had anything meaningful to offer a child.

But he wanted Natalie. So he was willing to try, or better yet, stay the hell out of the way so he didn't cause any emotional scars to the girl.

"I realize she's your priority," he said, trying to convey his willingness to accommodate. "But surely there are times when you have an evening free? When she's with her father?"

Natalie's eyes grew glossy as she stared at him. Her brow crinkled in a flinch and she looked down, bottom lip pouting out while she twisted her fingers in her lap.

"So that really is what you're suggesting? Except, rather than sneak around on your family, we should hide from mine."

"You're making it sound... No. Look, I can see why single parents don't want a revolving door of partners paraded in front of their child. If you want me to meet her, fine. I will." Even though it made him feel like he was offering to lock himself into the Mixed Marital Arts ring with the reigning champion. "I want to see you, Natalie. I've quit Makricosta's. There's no reason we can't date."

"The sex wasn't that good, Demitri. Find someone else," she dismissed with a fracture in her tone.

He had to check himself so he didn't leap out of his own skin.

"Do you need a *reminder*?" he challenged in a voice that rose with astonishment and dismay.

She shrank into her seat, giving him a helpless look not unlike the one she'd worn that first night when he'd dragged her into his room.

He remembered every single thing about every single encounter with her. Did she think that was normal?

Her brow crinkled with disgruntlement and she set her chin mutinously, but there was something incredibly vulnerable in her expression. She was trying to resist him and finding it hard. If he had any morals, he'd protect her against the lothario in him.

Damn it, he was so desperate to kiss her and *show* her…

Jamming a desultory foot against the opposite seat, he tilted back his head and groaned at the roof. Since when did he show mercy? Care? Use words to communicate rather than actions?

"I realize that walking out on you that night, when you took that call from her, was insulting," he said, searching for the right thing to say. "I've been regretting ever since that I didn't stay and try to find a compromise. I want to keep seeing you, Natalie. I like what we had. You told me you weren't looking for marriage and picket fences, either. Was that a lie?"

"No," she admitted after a weighty moment, voice low. "I have my own version of that already." She nosed toward the suburban street the limo had slowed to navigate.

It was a quaint old neighborhood of new mansions and restored heritage homes, mature trees and lopsided snowmen waving from the front yards. Not far from the city center, he noted. Quite the upscale location.

"Exactly how much does my brother pay you?" he asked.

She chuckled self-consciously. "My grandfather was an architect. He built the house and my mother inherited it, then it came to me. My mortgage paid for a new roof and some other updates along with the estate taxes, but the actual house was paid off years ago."

The limo turned into her drive and stopped. He leaned forward to look up at the charming two-story—three, since she appeared to have a basement. Steps rose to a covered and recessed front door. He liked how she'd married the 1940s architecture with efficient replica windows and modern siding.

"Invite me in to see it," he said as the chauffeur left to come around to her side.

She shook her head, gaze flicking to the back window of the limo. He glanced across the street to where a pair of little girls, bundled in snowsuits, climbed the berm of plowed snow to exclaim at the fancy car.

"Zoey walked home with her friend's mom, but will be hungry for dinner."

Inexplicably, he found himself about to insist she introduce him to her daughter, but he could already see the shadows of refusal building behind her eyes.

"When can *we* have dinner? Friday?" he asked, holding her pensive gaze. Willing her to capitulate.

She hesitated. "I don't know where this could go."

"Don't you?" he wanted to ask, but schooled himself from stealing a kiss to demonstrate.

She gave him a look that was a mixture of scold and hurt and yearning. Then she shot another look out the back window. "I have to go," she insisted, reaching for the door latch.

The moment she did, the chauffeur, who'd taken himself around to wait for her, opened her door.

"Friday," Demitri said, helping her gather her bags. "I'll be here at six."

"I..." Her attention was torn between him and the girl across the street. "I'll meet you in the city," she finally ceded.

He howled with triumph inside, but shook his head sternly. "You know my feelings on that. I'll be here."

She might have protested, but a happy cry of "Mom!" cut her off.

She straightened and urged the chauffeur to close the door, calling, "Stop and look for cars! Is it safe? Then yes, you can come across."

A moment later, she took a full-body hit in the middle from a girl with a purple hat and a yellow jacket who wrapped her arms around Natalie and beamed up at her. Her reddened nose topped a profile that was a rounder, younger version of Natalie's. He hadn't anticipated that she'd look like her mother, or have that same bright glow of optimism that he found so likable in Natalie.

"Why did you come home in this big car?" her high voice asked, audible through the glass. "Can I see inside?"

"A friend gave me a lift. How was school?" Natalie steered the girl to start up the front steps with her.

Natalie's daughter stopped and turned as the limo began to back out. She waved, but Natalie only watched, a troubled look on her face, bottom lip worried by her teeth.

Arriving home to find Zoey outside at the neighbor's had forestalled Natalie really working through everything that Demitri had said. She kept trying to tell herself that it didn't matter that he hadn't *meant* to hurt her. Or that, according to him, he hadn't used her, either. He thought what they'd had was *good*.

He still didn't want a future. He didn't want anything more than the casual arrangement they'd had in Paris. Actually, he wanted less, since he lived in New York. How would a relationship—an affair—even work? She definitely shouldn't cheapen herself by agreeing to one.

Except when he'd reminded her that she'd claimed not to want marriage and more children, an unexpected greed for *something* had risen in her. No, she wouldn't dare ask for the full package. Look how dreaming too big had stung her in Lyon. But it felt awfully good to have someone tell her she looked good, stroking her ego and her skin, before kissing her in a way that made her blood race.

Oh, she knew exactly what had happened. The charm train had rolled into the station and she was tempted to climb aboard, forgetting that she'd been dumped from it once before.

She agonized all day Thursday, then spent every spare moment on Friday drafting lies and excuses, going so far as to type them into her phone, but never hitting Send.

I have to work late.

I'll be in the city anyway.

I'm sick.

Zoey is sick.

Zoey was away for the weekend at her grandmother's. Yes, a wicked part of Natalie had wanted to be available to whatever Demitri might plan, but now that her workday was done and she was ruminating in front of her closet, she had to ask herself what the heck she thought she was doing.

She'd made her peace with being single after breaking up with Heath. Demitri had stirred up a pile of longings in her while they'd been in France, a vision she'd blacked out because it was so far-fetched, especially because it starred him. It would definitely be better if he disappeared as abruptly as he'd shown up.

Which was exactly what she'd tell him over dinner, she assured herself.

Then he showed up looking all alpha and sexy in a cream-colored mock turtleneck under a fitted blazer in chocolate brown. It had a casual formality that lent him authority and command. And he brought flowers and a bottle of wine, which nearly finished off whatever defenses she had.

"No chocolates?" she mused facetiously, trying not to melt into a puddle of submission.

He looked at the items in his hands, expression blanking with surprise. "They're in the limo."

"No way!" she burst out with a laugh. "I was joking."

He stared at her, making her self-conscious. A pleased, answering smile twitched his mouth. "That laugh gets me every time," he said, voice husky and intimate. Affected?

"I'll be right back." He pushed the wine and bouquet into her hands and left.

She did the only sensible thing she could do. She moved through to the kitchen to put the flowers in water, using them as a shield of busywork so he didn't completely disarm her when he returned.

Snowflakes glittered in his hair when he came back. He set a large, flat wooden box on the kitchen table.

Her eyes popped when she saw the gold-embossed name. He'd bought them a pair of those truffles from a specialty shop in Switzerland as if it was penny candy, even though he'd turned over a very large note for them. Eating hers had been a peak life experience. Now he'd brought her a whole *box* of them?

Shrugging out of his jacket, he draped it over the back of a chair and reached for the wine, beginning to peel the foil off the neck. "You look fantastic."

"Tickets, please," the conductor said, and she found herself with one foot on the Demitri Heartbreak Express, all of her tingling with excitement.

Check yourself, Natalie. Where on earth did she think this train was going? This wasn't France and fancy-free time. This was nine-to-five, get-the-groceries, be-a-mother-and-set-a-decent-example time. Sure, he had money and turned up with fringe benefits, but she couldn't count on him any more than she could on Heath.

"I bought it in Lyon," she said of the dress. She'd found it on one of her many excursions out of the hotel to avoid all those speculative looks. *Remember that?* she scolded herself.

The dress was a thick knit that fell to just above her knees, the wool speckled with green-and-gold tones. She'd paired it with a filmy gold scarf and a narrow belt. Her tall boots, pretty much her regulation attire from November to February, would jazz it up, but it wasn't deliberately sexy or seductive. She might as well be in a bikini, though, given the way he scoped her from top to bottom and back.

"The chauffeur is waiting, isn't he?" she hazarded as he opened a drawer in search of her corkscrew.

"I pay him very well to do exactly that."

Of course he did. Nipping the ends off the stems in the arrangement, she set the whole thing into her largest vase and filled it with water.

"How, if you don't mind my asking? There was an announcement that you'd left Makricosta. Did I get you fired?"

"No, I did that all by myself," he assured her, opening a cupboard at random, forcing her to point out the correct one. "Actually, it was a mutual parting of ways. I've wanted to leave for a while, but didn't feel right about it." He carefully positioned two glasses on the table. "I'm starting my own firm, so I can pick the jobs that interest me." He lifted a dark look at her that was vaguely insulted, but amused, too. "So I'm temporarily unemployed, but I'm not here to couch surf at an old flame's if that's what you're thinking."

She bit her lips together, suspecting she was being chastised for her man-child remark. "So I shouldn't feel guilty about the way you left? You and Adara have made up?"

"No," he said shortly. "I mean, no, you shouldn't feel guilty. My leaving was a long time coming, and no, my family isn't speaking to me right now." He poured and offered her a glass. "But I'm angry with them, too, so the radio silence is also a mutual thing."

She dried her hands and accepted the glass of chilled, lightly sparkling rosé, glancing up at him with concern.

He offered a blithe smile, uncaring, always trying to pretend he was superficial and lazy, spoiled and arrogant, but he had so much more going on below the surface.

"Demitri…" This would be a massive invasion of privacy, going a lot deeper than any conversation they'd delved into in Europe, but she felt she had to know. It was the reason he'd ended things so abruptly in Switzerland. Searching his eyes, she asked, "What makes you so averse to family? What happened with yours? Why are you so angry?"

His lips thinned, rejecting her question, gearing up to refuse to answer, she thought.

"They kept something from me," he surprised her by replying. "Until a few years ago, I didn't know that I—we—have an older brother. Half brother." He tilted his glass, staring into it so hard it should have sizzled and boiled dry. "Nic Marcussen."

"Nic… *The* Nic Marcussen? The media guy? Who owns, like, half the world's magazines and news channels?"

"Yes." He sipped, blinking to contain what she sensed were volatile emotions.

"That's quite a secret big brother."

"Right?" he challenged, fury creeping like lava under his tone.

"Why didn't they tell you?"

"*I don't know.* But he's back in our lives—their lives—and I don't know what the hell I'm supposed to do with that, so I've been keeping my distance." He set aside his glass, pushing his hands into his pants' pockets broodingly. "Adara seems to think we should all get together in some sort of family reunion. I've been resisting, finding other things to do, which annoys her. That's why she thought I was using you to get at her and Theo, but I'm not *that* childish. I just don't want anything to do with him."

Not all families were as close as she'd been to her mother and brother. She knew that, but it still made her sad for him and his siblings. And keeping such a huge secret was a curious mystery that made her want to quiz him further, but he changed the subject.

"Show me around. Is this flooring maple?"

* * *

Thankfully Natalie could take a hint. She took him upstairs for a brief glance in the three bedrooms, a tidy master just airy and pastel enough to confirm it belonged to a woman.

"Queen," he commented, eyeing the mattress, thinking it would do.

"Because my daughter sneaks in," she said with a don't-even-think-it smile.

He was thinking it. Of course he was. That dress she was wearing was a statement in subtle eroticism, clinging to her curves in a mysterious way that hinted while hiding, driving him insane with desire to press and feel and stroke.

He let her take him along to the princess-themed girl's room full of stuffed animals and well-stocked bookshelves, and then another bedroom converted to her home office.

His interest in the house had been piqued from his first glimpse. He'd thought it was basic curiosity in things like architecture and workmanship, but he realized he'd really wanted this glimpse into Natalie's true self. He wanted to know why she held such a grip on him. Despite her sunny nature, she kept a lot of herself private. Her child, for instance.

Her office was as efficient and practical as he knew her to be on the job, but the framed child's artwork down the stairs and newspaper article above the fireplace congratulating her grandparents on their fiftieth wedding anniversary reflected her less obvious, but very endearing qualities: warmth and sentimentality and hints of a romantic.

"The dining room is a mess. I've taken up scrapbooking." She flicked on the light, but hung back as though she'd rather he didn't enter.

"You know you can do that sort of thing on computer now?" He purposefully brushed past her through the arched doorway, taking advantage of the movement to graze a light touch on her shoulder and upper arm, liking the way she jumped under his caress.

"I spend all day on computers. I like doing something real. Don't look. You're Mr. Marketing and Ad Campaign. I'll never measure up," she protested, catching up a handful of crumpled paper in a tight fist.

When they called it scrap, they meant it. The table was covered in bits of colored paper, buttons and ribbons, and novelty stickers, but the chaos was nothing he hadn't seen on his own desk when he needed a cut-and-paste mock-up.

"You have a good eye for composition," he said sincerely, taken with a collage of black-and-white snapshots of her grandparents that she'd arranged with silver borders on a sheet of pale green.

"It's, um—" she edged protectively toward a finished book "—just something to do with all my mom's boxes of photographs."

He spied the photo on the front of the finished book, a baby in an incubator. Something in the colors of the snapshot told him it was real, not a print from digital. Older. He set his hand on the book to draw it across the cloth on the table so it was before him. "Gareth," he read. "Your brother?"

"Yes, it's…" Her hand wavered as she decided whether to stop him opening the cover. "I wanted something that Zoey could keep, so he's not forgotten."

Her voice had gone husky. He could tell she wasn't comfortable with letting him see, but he couldn't resist turning the pages, admiring the care she'd taken with designing each page, but more ensnared by the story she told.

Natalie had said her father had left, and there was no evidence of him here. As for her brother, he had spent his life in hospital and sick beds, occasionally a sofa or a picnic blanket. Her wearily smiling mom was usually behind the camera rather than in front of it, capturing her underweight but grinning son and his vibrant, obviously devoted older sister. In the early ones Natalie cuddled and coddled him; as they grew up, she did terrible things to his hair with clips and bows. She made faces at him over a hand of cards, sat with him in front of a bin of building blocks and eventually aligned herself behind a computer screen next to him.

That was where her interest in IT had come from, Demitri would bet. She couldn't throw a ball with this boy. She would have had to race him in video games.

"You told me your brother had died, but I didn't realize he'd been sick all his life." He looked at her with new eyes, amazed by how effervescent she often was after everything her small family must have endured. "What was it?"

"A congenital heart defect, but there were other things that came along with it."

"Was it…" He could see her shutting down. "You don't want to talk about it. Too painful?" Of course it was.

She nod-shrugged. "I don't mind talking about him, but his illness was my whole life for so long… That sounds awful." She shrugged jerkily. "As if I resent him, and I don't. But my entire childhood revolved around his appointments and surgeries and recoveries and lack of a future. Everything that needed to be said about his condition was said while he was alive. The only important piece now is that I loved him."

She stroked his image, her smile brave and crooked, causing something to shift in his chest. It hurt and made him reach out, drawing her in so he could soothe.

"Oh, Nat," he murmured, setting a hand on her silky hair, tucking her crown under his chin in an unfamiliar need to comfort. "And then you lost your mom."

"She was tired," Natalie said on a breath of sorrow, dropping her hand onto his waist, not quite accepting his embrace, but he thought it might be more about fighting her own emotions. Her voice wasn't steady. "She fought for Gareth every day. Urged him to keep fighting, and took on the system that didn't expect him to make it past two or three years old. If there was a treatment or surgery we hadn't tried, she made it happen. Then he was gone and I was married, and I think she thought she could rest. She didn't have to worry about either of us. I went away with Heath just after Zoey was born, up to his mother's farm, and Mom got the flu."

Natalie drew away, brushing fingertips under her eyes where her makeup was threatening to run. "She'd had enough of hospitals." She closed Gareth's book and set it aside, as though she was trying to set aside her grief. "She wouldn't even go to the doctor. I came home and got her admitted, but she had pneumonia by then and it killed her."

And Natalie's husband hadn't come to the funeral.

"I'm so sorry, Natalie."

She gave a muted shrug. "She's with Gareth now. We should go, shouldn't we?"

Her defenseless expression bordered on persecuted. She needed time to regroup the way he had after talking about Nic.

He didn't want to leave. He wanted to hold her again. Touching her had felt good. Right.

They were both raw from delving into things that he was still shocked he'd revealed, though. And getting physical right now would be less about the kind of escape he longed for and could take the intimacy of their conversation to an unforgettably deep level. Something he couldn't come back from.

"Probably a good idea," he agreed, following her to the front door and watching her zip into shiny black spiked-heel boots that hugged her calves and cocked her curves into a sassy posture when she straightened. That backside of hers never quit. Shame to cover it, but he held her coat and drank in the scent of creamy vanilla in her hair, so familiar he forgot for a moment where he was. Things in him that had been wound tight relaxed. A smile touched his lips as he thought about brushing aside her blond tresses and setting his lips on her nape.

She went still, and he glanced up to see they faced a mirror. He stood behind her and to the right, not unlike the photo of her grandparents. Whether she'd seen his expression of desire, or saw the similarity to the longtime couple's pose, he didn't know, but he found himself taking a mental snapshot of the two of them looking at each other so nakedly, his hands on her shoulders, her expression still shadowed by emotion, his own filled with tender affection.

It struck him that you didn't get to fifty years by staying detached. You shared the things next to your soul. In his previous life, he wouldn't have encouraged her to give him the details of her most terrible heartaches. But it hurt him to see her suffer. He wanted to hear what pained her so he could carry some of the burden for her.

Disturbed, he looked away, feeling her pull away from his light touch at the same time.

Natalie was changing him. He didn't understand why or how, but he'd felt it after their breakup, sitting in New York unable to stop thinking about her.

In the car, he studied what he could see of her profile in the dark silence, trying to work it out, wondering if there was a Freudian element to it.

"Did you have to look after your brother a lot?" he asked her.

"Yes," she said simply, adding, "when Mom went to work, which was three nights a week and every weekend. Someone had to make sure he took his meds or monitor his temperature and pulse if he was recovering from surgery. Mom was spread so thin, I did a lot of the housekeeping and cooking, too. Then I had Heath and Zoey to look after. I still have to remind Heath to pay his rent," she said with a little tsk. "I've never *not* felt responsible for someone. That's why, well, it's what I was taking a vacation from," she admitted in a small voice. "In France."

He could help her carry some of that load.

"How old were you when it started? When you had to be a little mom to your brother?" he asked.

"I don't know. After Dad left, I guess. Seven? Gareth would have been three."

He rubbed his thigh, confiding family secrets before he lost his nerve. "Adara was younger than that when she started looking after me. Five or six."

Natalie turned her head, voice colored with surprise when she said, "Really? Where was your mom? Working?"

"Passed out." He could still see the unresponsive shape in her bed. When Theo had called him to tell him she was gone, he'd had to catch back a tasteless, "Are we sure this time?" because he'd thought her dead so many times as a child.

"She liked to wash down her pills with vodka. Dad liked to drink, too," he stated flatly. Then he closed his eyes and walked through the door he'd only peeked through that day by the pool with Theo. "He got violent when he'd had enough of it. If Adara didn't keep me quiet, she got smacked. If Theo failed, he caught Dad's belt."

"Oh, my God." Natalie caught her gasp with her cupped hand, understandably speechless. Her eyes glowed white at the edges, not that he was able to meet her gaze for long.

Why had he been so cavalier that day with Theo? It had been cruel, and he didn't blame his brother for not returning the one call he'd placed to try to make amends. The truth was he didn't understand why his brother hadn't rejected him the moment it had happened.

Demitri never looked back on his childhood. Ever. But

he made himself remember that incident now. Made himself feel the guilt. He'd left his room, even though Theo had tried to stop him, but Demitri had been determined to find Adara. Not their mother. His sister. Because Adara had been the one he relied on. She'd been the closest thing to a mother he'd had while theirs had been a slurring mess who'd rarely left her bedroom.

And Theo had taken the punishment for Demitri's transgression.

Who *did* that to a little kid? Why hadn't someone called child services?

Why hadn't *he* been the one to catch hell?

Fierce, angry tears came into his eyes so hard and fast he had to avert his face to the window and remind himself he'd been three years younger than Theo's eight. He hadn't really known what he'd been doing. He had barely understood what had been happening when Theo had screamed in their father's den. It was only later, when Adara had pleaded with him, "You have to be good, Demitri," that he'd begun to comprehend that Theo's injuries, the stripes on his back that were visible to this day, had been his fault.

And despite Adara's pleading, he'd never been good. He didn't think he ever would be.

CHAPTER EIGHT

"AND YOU?" NATALIE asked with trepidation, lowering her hand, needing to know, to understand him, but certain she wouldn't be able to withstand whatever she heard.

Demitri shook his head, expression impossible to read.

"He loved me." He made a quick noise of negation, clarifying in a bitter tone, "I mean, he loved to throw me at Adara and Theo in ugly little ways. 'Demitri got a trophy today, Theo. What did you get?' 'Have you fed your brother today, Adara? Why are you eating if he hasn't?'"

Natalie couldn't move. A cry of denial that anyone could put children through such mental and physical torture locked her throat.

"That's really horrible," she managed.

"It's sick," he hissed, revealing a pressure of anger he suspected had been bottled tight for years. "I *tried* to make him hit me. I dented his car and drank his booze, skipped school and broke the front window. He was the only one home that day, half a bottle in him. It wasn't even lunch. Winter. Snow was blowing in. You know what he said? 'Call Theo. Tell him to come home and fix it.' That's crazy, right? Like, legitimately not sane?"

Finally he looked at her, and while his brow was an anguished line, his eyes were glazed with wrath. The devil-may-care veneer was cracked wide-open, revealing that the man inside did care about things. He cared a lot.

"Demitri, I'm so sorry," she could only say, while the back of her throat stung.

The car stopped.

He seemed to shake himself out of his past. "I shouldn't have told you that."

She reached out to cover his hand, folding her fingers over his stiff ones. "It's okay." She got the feeling he'd never told anyone. "Did no one ever report him?"

He shook his head, turning his face forward, but his hand shifted in hers so he could pinch her fingers in a tight grip. It was as though he was holding on to a lifeline so he wouldn't be sucked under and drowned.

"We had money. The privilege of the rich extends to not having your actions questioned. I've learned that. Even when you're leaving marks on your kids, you can get away with it. I remember waiting for Adara at school one day. Her teacher told her she could stay in class as long as she wanted, but Adara told her it was better if she got me home on time. The teachers knew. They didn't do anything."

"You never thought about making a call yourself?"

The corner of his mouth twisted. "By the time I realized I could, I'd developed my own way of dealing with it. The old man would be reaching for Adara and I'd spill my milk. Instead of shaking her, he'd tell her to mop it up. Then we all grew into teenagers and Theo was big enough that Dad kept most of his bullying to verbal. Even at that, it never stopped. And they took it! It made me so crazy." His hand worked hers with hard agitation, but she ignored the discomfort, sensing this was a much-needed bleeding out of poison. "I'd say, 'Just tell him no,' and Theo wouldn't even hear me. He'd just keep doing whatever he'd been told to do. He took accounting! The man should be engineering fighter jets."

Natalie could hardly take in all she was hearing. She had grown up sad and frustrated with her brother's illness, but aside from resentment over her father leaving, their house had been loving. So loving.

She didn't know how anyone could live with something so twisted and painful. No wonder the Makricostas were standoffish and hard to read.

"And they never hated me, no matter how bad it got for them. No matter what I did. I slept with Theo's fiancée, for God's sake!" He glared at her, half his face lit by the slant of neon glow from the street, making him look satanic as he practically insisted she revile him for his actions.

"With *Jaya*?" Her mind started to explode, but he quickly dismissed that.

"No. Long before her. Someone Dad arranged." His grip on her hand eased. "I knew Theo didn't want to go through with it and asked him why he didn't just leave. He was in his twenties. I couldn't understand why he was still letting Dad run his life, and Theo said, 'If I don't get married, Adara will have to.' We'd seen the kind of Neanderthals Dad was trying to fix her up with. She was trying so hard, even that late in the day, to make us look like a nuclear family, never acknowledging that it was radioactive. I could see why Theo was willing to make the sacrifice, but I couldn't let him go through with it. So I slept with his fiancée and that broke them up. Then Adara married Gideon and I honestly don't know why Theo stuck around after that. To make sure Gideon was good to her, maybe."

"You could try asking him," she suggested gently.

He snorted. "I told you. They're not talking to me."

He rapped a knuckle on the window and the chauffeur opened his door. Demitri reached back to help her out, then hugged her into his side as he walked her into the restaurant.

They were both shivering, and she wasn't sure how much was cold and how much was reaction. Never in her wildest imaginings had she seen such a history on him.

It explained a lot, but raised more questions, most pressingly: Where were they going?

Not for their date, of course. She could see he'd brought her to Old Montreal. They entered a converted industrial building where they were ushered through a trendy lounge to an elevator. It opened into an elegant space of velvet chairs and crystal chandeliers, where a table had been reserved against the windows overlooking the St. Laurence.

But where were they going as a couple?

As they were seated she saw far too many similarities to their first meal. The waiter set her napkin in her lap and Demitri ordered wine and a mixed plate of seafood hors d'oeuvres for them to share.

Of course, she'd told him in Paris that she liked lobster and shellfish, and this place had a reputation for offering the finest of both. Perhaps he was being less high-handed and more thoughtful than she gave him credit for?

Linking her fingers together, she touched her knuckles to her lips, elbows braced on the table, and regarded him through the tangle of her lashes, intrigued by the dance of light and shadow from the candle flame against the carved angles of his handsome face.

"What are you thinking?" he prompted.

"Honestly? I doubt you've ever told anyone what you've told me tonight. I'm wondering, why me?"

His lip curled in self-contempt. "If you only knew how many times I've listened to some rejected pop diva or a humiliated politician going through a divorce. 'Thanks for listening,' they always say, while I shake my head at their bizarre desire to share their personal garbage. I have no idea, Natalie. I felt like I *could* tell you, I suppose."

She smiled wistfully, not entirely surprised. "I'm easy to talk to because I'm used to having the hard conversations. I never had the luxury of radio silence with my brother."

He looked up sharply.

"I didn't mean that to sound superior," she said with an apologetic quirk of her mouth. "I can see why your family would avoid talking about your childhood, but…" She leaned forward. "What if something happened, Demitri? Do you really want this animosity sitting unresolved between you forever?"

His face spasmed briefly and he looked to the window.

After a long minute, after she'd retreated into her chair and tucked her hands in her lap, he said, "No. Of course not."

He shifted, gave his jaw a brief skim with his hand.

"That first day we met? Gideon accosted me right after you'd spoken to him. He was pressing me to come to Adara's birthday party. I was annoyed and took it out on you. I don't want to go. Nic will be there." He grimaced. "But I keep thinking I should. It would mean a lot to her."

"You really don't remember him? I find that so strange. How is he even…? Did your father have an affair?"

"How sexist of you, Natalie," Demitri scolded. "My mother had the affair. My parents had broken their engagement and she had a fling with Nic's dad, from what I've been told. Then she got back together with our father and passed off the baby as his. Maybe she even believed it. She was pregnant with me when Dad realized Nic wasn't his. They sent him to boarding school. I guess we saw him a handful of times after that, but the closest thing I have to a memory of him is asking Dad, 'Who's Nic?' I don't know why it came up or who else was in the room. I just remember the look on his face and being scared. I was sure I was going to get it. Then he slapped me on the back and laughed."

"Your father punished them for remembering him," she said on a wisp of stunned disbelief. "But not you, because you didn't."

His face fell in shock. Obviously it hadn't occurred to him.

"That's really cruel, Demitri," she said, numb with incredulity. "You're entitled to feel confused and angry. All of you are. I can't believe anyone would act that way toward their own children."

"I always had a kind of survivor's guilt, because they suffered and I didn't." He frowned at the table. "I always thought I should have been punished the way they were. I looked for the line. I pushed and pushed to find it. And I always figured they should hate me because I wasn't catching hell the way they were. Now they do hate me, and even though I deserve it—"

The sommelier arrived with their wine, giving them both time to regain their composure.

"You should go to her party," she told him when they were alone again. "You don't have to get into all of this, but at least turn up."

He only gave her a disgruntled look, as though he knew she was right but was reluctant to admit it. Then his attention on her sharpened. He narrowed his eyes, holding her gaze with that willpower of his that was so implacable.

"Come with me."

"What? No," she said decisively, and then had to ask, "Why would you even suggest it?"

"Because we're seeing each other."

"No, we're not! We're having dinner," she insisted. "Once. Tonight. So I can tell you we're not doing this again."

Demitri sat back, face icing into hard angles. "Because you're afraid I'll turn out like my old man?"

"What? No!" The protest came out unreservedly. He was as capable as anyone of saying something awful, obviously, and far too used to getting his own way, but the times she'd seen him angry, he'd been tightly controlled, not one to resort to violence.

"I've cut way back on my drinking," he continued as if he hadn't heard her. "Not that I was ever a mean drunk. I hate losing my temper. I wouldn't so much as raise my voice to you. Are you afraid for Zoey?"

She could see genuine agony in him. Perhaps the only glimpse anyone would ever get of him with shaken confidence.

Natalie shook her head emphatically. "I don't think you would ever hurt me or Zoey. But, Demitri, that woman you met in Paris, that's not me. You won't find me as fun or accessible as I was. I can't play pretend again."

Demitri was feeling his way on very thin ice. Relief had deflated a lifelong tension in him as he realized that his father hadn't favored him because he saw something of himself in his son. That black mark on his soul was lifting, thanks to Natalie's insight, but it didn't mean he was reformed into the kind of man who would fit into her life. He respected that she'd engineered her personal world so she was self-sufficient. He admired her for it. And God knew he had never measured up to anyone's expectations unless they were basement level. He didn't blame her for her lack of willingness to take a chance on him.

But if there was a way he could keep seeing her, he wanted to find it.

"What do you want from a man, Natalie?"

"Why do you think I need anything from a man?" she challenged lightly.

"You don't need *anything*?" he asked with a skeptical cock of his brow. He swept her blushing cheeks with a masculine gaze of interest that hovered on lips she nervously dampened with her tongue.

"You seduced me in France because I allowed it," she asserted, adding blithely, "I can seduce myself if I want to."

"Flirt," he accused, delighted when she was cheeky and

suggestive. "You know I'd like to see that." She never, ever bored him. He adored that about her.

"I'm not flirting," she lied, mouth twitching with rueful amusement.

"It was a challenge, then?"

"No," she said firmly. "And don't think for a minute I don't know how to say that word when I need to."

"Cute of you to think so, but you're the biggest soft touch going, Natalie."

"I have a daughter to think of," she countered with a shift in her mood to grave sincerity. "As weak as I might be as a woman, as a mother I would lift cars and tear grown men apart to protect her. That's what I'm trying to say, Demitri. That's who I am here. Mom first. Woman second."

He pondered that, asking cautiously, "Do you want a father for her?"

"She has one," she said with a pragmatic shrug. "He's not perfect, but she gets more from him than I got from mine."

"Love, you mean." The word hurt to say because it was an emotion so foreign and incomprehensible to him, he doubted he could ever offer such a thing.

Natalie didn't laugh or mock. She didn't light up and say yes. She pursed her mouth as though trying to school her lips from trembling. He watched her throat work as she swallowed, and he sensed pain. It made his throat hurt.

"Love is nice," she said with a flicker of a smile. "But it doesn't mean anything. Heath tells me he loves me all the time. I still can't live with him."

"Does he?" Demitri began to fall, pushed so abruptly into a chasm of darkness he couldn't see or feel or breathe.

"He says it after he feeds Zoey junk food all day, or gets her from school but forgets her backpack. As if he's this great guy capable of loving me even though I'm angry with him. I thought my father loved me and he left because life got hard. Love isn't enough. I want someone I can count on."

She looked up at him, but he couldn't reply. What could he say? They both knew Demitri Makricosta could only be counted on to do what he shouldn't.

"Natalie…" He found himself laughing bitterly at what a mess this had become. He'd flown up here thinking he could fall into bed with her and stop feeling this angst and dismay with his life. Instead, he was baring his soul in a fight for a place in her life. "The way I've always behaved… I don't want to be that man anymore."

The persona he'd cultivated had worn thin even with him. No one ever gave him credit for the level of control he exerted, and he was tired of being underestimated.

"I can appreciate that, Demitri. I can," she said, so earnestly she moved him, giving him hope yet gently rejecting him. "But I can't afford to be your guinea pig. I can't invest my time and heart, my *daughter's* heart, while you figure out if you really want to stick around."

Was she asking for a deeper level of commitment? Marriage?

The thought should have put him firmly on the run, ending dinner before they'd eaten the appetizer that arrived with a waft of buttery garlic and salty tang.

He wasn't repelled by the idea of marriage to her, though. He liked sharing space with her, waking next to her, eating across from her. In France, he'd wanted to make her his mistress, but he could easily see something more permanent. Given how hard she'd had it, he would feel really good if she'd let him provide for her.

The stumbling block was her daughter. Maybe Natalie didn't expect a father for Zoey, but he would never convince her to let him infiltrate *her* small family if he remained estranged from his own.

* * *

Natalie picked at food so exquisitely prepared she ought to be moaning aloud, but her heart was weighted by Demitri's silence and everything tasted like cardboard in her mouth.

When their waiter came to remove the plates and ask after the next course, she was surprised that Demitri ordered entrées. He'd gone so quiet she had assumed the date was over.

"Really?" she asked when the waiter had left. "I thought you might want to call it a night."

"Natalie," he chided. "When I said I want to change, it doesn't mean I've lost my taste for getting what I want. I won't slink away and die because you expressed a few doubts about my reliability. Count on me to be persistent, at least."

She shouldn't laugh at that, but a mixture of relief and alarm twitched her lips.

He intended to *pursue* her. The scent of danger sharpened in her nose and her heart rate kicked up. She shook her head, fearful she wouldn't be strong enough to resist him if he had his mind set on possessing her.

She wanted to be possessed. Therein lay the problem.

"Don't make this hard for me, Demitri." It was a plea.

He picked up her hand, smiling ruefully as he drew it across the table and leaned forward to kiss her knuckles. "I could say the same to you."

He was asking her to allow him to break her heart. She *must* be the biggest soft touch going, because she sat there and let him continue to hold her hand, incapable of arguing.

"How's work?" he asked, taking her by surprise. "Catch me up on the gossip."

"Seriously?" she asked with a disconcerted laugh. "Why?"

"We've had enough of the hard conversations for now,

haven't we? Let's remind ourselves why we enjoyed each other so much in Paris. Tell me if that idiot Laurier is still rewriting all of my carefully worded campaigns when he translates them into French. That always annoyed the hell out of me."

Oh, he was a magnetic man. Far too capable of disarming and engaging. She found herself admitting, "Laurier's losing his mind at all the shake-ups in that department since you left, thinking he ought to have been promoted over Sanjit."

They wound their way through a million topics over dinner, taking their time, lingering over specialty coffee and crème brulée while the restaurant emptied. When he said, "Tell me about Zoey," she hesitated.

"What do you want to know?"

"Anything you would have told me in France if you hadn't been afraid to."

She shrugged, thinking of all the moments she'd almost said, "One time Zoey..." Wrinkling her nose, she admitted, "Last week she asked me where babies come from."

"Wow," he said, chuckling at the wry panic she recreated for him. "What did you say? Stork or cabbage patch?"

"I was close to my mom because she was always honest with me," she said with a helpless lift of her hand. "I had to tell her. It was a very basic version, of course. I skimmed over *a lot*."

He grinned at her, so much admiration in his look she had to glance away from the intensity of its glow.

"You're a good mom, Natalie. Contrary to what I made you think our last night in Switzerland, it's actually one of your most appealing qualities."

Tears sprang to her eyes and she swallowed, deeply moved. She tried really hard to be a good mom, wished daily that she had her own mother to ask for advice and second-guessed herself all the time. Demitri was hardly an expert, but it still meant a lot to her that he'd said that. No one ever did.

"Thank you," she murmured shyly.

"I would never try to get between you. I hope you believe that," he said solemnly. "What you have with her is precious. I'd do everything I could to preserve it."

Perhaps he wasn't an expert on good parenting, but he was very well versed in terrible. The flimsy defenses she had against him wavered and fluttered like the walls on a house of cards.

"I should pay before they turn the lights out on us," he said, reaching into his pocket.

A few minutes later, he held her chair and kept his hand at her back as he steered her toward the door. His touch sizzled through her dress and she knew there was only one way she wanted this evening to end.

Weak, weak Natalie. Was he playing her in his expert way, seducing her to his will? Or was this real?

When he'd helped her with her coat earlier, she'd caught a look so tender on his face, she'd been completely beguiled. Still, it surprised her when he turned her in the elevator and made no effort to disguise the warmth and desire in his gaze. He curled his fists into her lapels, then paused as though waiting for permission.

She looked at his mouth and licked her lips, sexual yearning swirling into her middle as she anticipated his kiss. "Yes, please," she heard herself whisper, and cringed inwardly at how blatant and needy that sounded.

He reacted with a look of aching hunger and lowered his head, covering her mouth with the hot mastery of his own. Where she expected to be crushed, he caressed, then gradually deepened the kiss into the sort of seductive coaxing he was so devastatingly good at delivering.

Her breath shuddered out in a warm hiss against his cheek and she leaned into him, increasing the pressure of their kiss, encouraging him to gently and thoroughly ravage her. Relearning all the hard muscles of his back and shoulders beneath his open jacket.

He made a growled, grateful noise in his throat that the staff must have heard, because the elevator had opened just then. She didn't care any more than he seemed to. He delicately plundered for every last dreg of her response and she gave it to him, recognizing that she'd been aching for this since four-fifteen outside the hotel two days ago. Since about five minutes after he'd walked out of the room they'd been sharing in Switzerland.

The doors started to close, and they reluctantly eased back, loosening the death grip they'd taken on each other. He stopped the door, but kept his gaze locked to hers. Her blood continued to sizzle in her arteries and she had to consciously lock her trembling knees. No way could she look at anyone as they exited, fingers linked, breaths hot enough to cloud the winter air as they climbed into the limo.

"Are you spending the night with me?" she asked in the safety of the darkened car. She refused to ask—beg— *will* you?

"I want to," he said, head turning toward her as he spoke.

She heard the unspoken *but*, and her heart went into free fall. This was why she had accepted their casual relationship in Paris. The minute she expected more from him, she risked being grossly disappointed.

"But?" she prompted, trying to pull her hand away from his warm grip.

He tightened his hold. "But if I spend the night, I spend the weekend. And next weekend, you come to New York and Adara's party with me."

She'd already told him Zoey was away until Sunday night, but "Next weekend I have Zoey. I can't go away."

This was precisely what she'd been trying to warn him about. She wasn't footloose and fancy—

"She can come. You have a passport for her, don't you?"

"I…" She did, and she was saving up to take her to the amusement parks in Florida, but "That's not the point."

"It's not any kind of point. We don't have to sleep together in New York if you think it would confuse her. Share the spare room in my apartment with her or I'll get you a hotel room if you prefer. And I'll pay for the flights. You won't be out of pocket."

"Demitri, I can't," she protested, forced to bring up the real issue. "There's no way I could throw myself, *us*, in your family's faces like that."

"What does that mean? You're embarrassed to be seen with me?"

"No! But our affair created a huge headache both at work and in their family life. The last person they want to see is the woman who caused it all."

"You didn't. I did. And I assure you, they'll be far more welcoming to you than they will be to me," he predicted in a rancorous mutter.

"They think I want to sue them for sexual harassment," she reminded, vehemently getting down to brass tacks.

"Exactly. And your turning up will reassure them that you're not holding a grudge."

She hadn't thought about it that way, but "It would still be awkward."

"Natalie," he said from between clenched teeth. "If I show up alone, Gideon will have me kicked out before I reach the elevator. If I have a date, someone he respects, he'll show some manners and give me a chance to apologize to my sister. You can rest assured that I will be bearing the brunt of the awkward."

"Still—"

"Damn it, Natalie. I don't like them thinking I was only

seeing you to hurt them. They were the last thing on my mind. I want them to see we're a serious couple."

Was that what they were?

Because she strongly suspected that was what she was really shying away from, she acknowledged darkly to herself. It was one thing to invite him in for the night, relive the fantasy and feel desired for a few hours. It was quite another to let a man occupy a more permanent space in her life. She might start to depend on him. Want stuff. Yearn for love and completion and other things that she secretly feared were never meant to be hers.

They didn't speak again until the car parked in her driveway. Demitri climbed out to walk her to her door, where he lightly cupped her face and said, "I can tell you want time—"

"No," she interrupted, grasping at his arm where he lightly touched her jaw. "If there's one thing Gareth taught me, it's that time is finite. Tomorrow might not come. You have to live today as best you can. I want you to stay. I do."

"Yeah?" His touch on her gentled and he drew her forward so he could press his lips to her forehead.

She closed her eyes, enjoying the simple gesture for a moment before drawing away with a smile and opening her front door. She stepped through and held it, inviting him in.

He hung back, making her frown in confusion.

"I'll just get my bag," he said.

"Of course you have a bag," Natalie snarked when he returned. She had the box of chocolates open and was unwrapping a truffle. She glared at him as she bit into it.

He stopped in his tracks, recognizing that perhaps there was something distasteful in the fact that he'd thrown it into the car without really thinking about it, packing it as routinely as he had a thousand times when leaving for an evening with a woman he desired. But her condemnation caught him off guard, making him shoot back, "It's called being prepared. Do you want me to get you pregnant?"

She paled and choked, covering her mouth before chewing and swallowing audibly. Closing the foil on the truffle, she placed it back in the box and said a firm "No."

For some reason that stung, even though it hadn't been a real question. He'd meant tonight, not *someday*, but her answer seemed to encompass both. It was a painful rejection.

He cursed and ran a hand over his hair, knowing what the real problem was here.

"I've slept with other women," he said flatly, continuing despite the injured glance she flashed at him. "But I've never slept with anyone who knows anything about me. If you think this is something I do all the time, it's not. Getting naked with someone is easy when you feel like the smartest, strongest, least-invested person in the room. I don't right now. Not with you." He glared at her, resenting how much guilt accosted him over those easy, meaningless hook-ups when he realized what he wanted from her. "I don't want sex from you, Natalie. I want to feel you and smell you and be inside you. I want to know you're mine."

He looked like a pirate. A sultan. A marauder bent on stealing her from her home. Or, at the very least, stealing her heart from her body.

"I'm scared," she admitted. "I don't want to start believing you'll be here and then find out the hard way that you won't." He hadn't even met Zoey. How could he be so sure they were a *serious* couple when he hadn't really seen her as a mom?

He opened his hands, coming forward to take her elbows as she draped her fingers on his biceps, surrounding her in his masculine scent and aura of command. "I don't know how to reassure you except to be here when you wake up."

Of their own accord, her fingertips moved restlessly on the stiff fabric of his jacket, wanting the man beneath.

He read her receptiveness in the betraying little motion.

He slid his hand down her forearm, linking their fingers as he canted his head toward the stairs. "Take me up with you."

This was how he did it, she thought as she led him to her room. He made her think she was in control when he was the one guiding the whole thing. Except, as they started to undress each other, he watched her closely, not rushing her, seeing if his caress against the side of her breast was welcome, stealing a kiss, but a soft, sweet one.

And when they were almost naked, he gathered her against his hard chest with arms that trembled and said, "I've missed you, Natalie."

"I can tell," she teased, trying to lighten the mood because she was so moved. She shifted a hand between them so she could caress the fierce muscle straining between them.

He closed his hand over hers, stilling her with a firm crush of his grip over hers. Then he caught her other hand and drew both her arms behind her so he could manacle her wrists. "My turn," he warned, fingertips playing against the lace triangle at the front of her panties, making her flinch with sensitivity. "Uh-uh," he scolded. "Stand still."

She bit her lips, whimpering as he slowly eased her panties down just enough to expose her to the tracing pad of his fingertip, delicately teasing her damp flesh into blossoming open, welcoming a deeper caress. "Demitri," she gasped, her vision going white as he aroused her with deliberate expertise.

"You were like this that first time. So wet. As if you couldn't wait for me to be inside you. I wanted to lick into this heat, but I couldn't wait, either." He pressed her backward onto the bed, releasing her hands so she splayed them, trying to keep her balance as he tipped her against the edge, skimming her undies from her legs and throwing them away. Then he knelt and pressed her knees open. "This time I will."

"Demitri—"

He draped her thighs over his shoulders, pulling her into the tender plunder of his kiss, demanding everything from her, making her abdomen knot into such tension she nearly screamed, then releasing her to such a burst of pleasure she did cry out, arching and throwing back her head with abandon, willpower demolished. Subjugated by passion into a vessel for his pleasure.

He rose to roll on a condom, taking a moment to study her utter abandonment before he covered her. Very much the marauder taking his slave. He caged her with his arms, all man, ferociously possessive. He drove into her with the thick flesh that her body had been aching for, pressing inexorably into her. It was the piece that she'd been missing, erasing the ache of solitude and filling her with joy.

Wrapping her legs around him, she pulled him in, accepting all of him, and he shut his eyes as if it was too much. He began to move and she closed her eyes, too, unable to bear the intimacy. It was too acute. He was taking something from her that she would never get back. Perhaps it was her heart. It might even be her soul.

For this kind of pleasure, this kind of closeness, she told herself it was worth it. She would give him anything, she dimly acknowledged, as long as he continued making her feel whole.

Demitri felt strange as he padded around Natalie's home barefoot and shirtless, sun streaming in through the front window to warm the hardwood floor. Last night had been intense, their appetites for each other as strong as ever and sharpened by emotion. Sex had been many things for him, usually escape or distraction, entertainment certainly. It had never been profound. It had never been a vehicle for closeness, for cementing a bond.

He kept having flashes of exposure, thinking of the things he'd told Natalie about himself. Then he would remember the way she'd opened herself to him, allowing his greed and dominance in her bed, letting him regain his masculinity while stroking and encouraging him, praising him for the pleasure he gave her. Snuggling tight against him with complete trust.

Something in him had been terrified she would reject him for all he'd told her. Her acceptance of him was disconcerting and oddly healing. It had pushed him from the bed before he'd had a full night's sleep, restless to do more to close the gap between them. He'd sent a few emails and texts, looked in her refrigerator and settled for three truffles, then called a cab to deliver coffee and breakfast.

When it arrived, he threw on his jacket and shoes and ran out to pay, coming back to a locked door.

"Hey!" He glimpsed Natalie's form through the window and knocked his elbow against the glass, showing her the fast-food bags.

She opened the door, a cross look on her face. "I thought you were ducking out."

"Excuse me?" He was astonished, considering what he'd been up to this morning.

"Well, the coffeemaker is right there. You ate three of my truffles," she accused.

"So you locked me out? Even though my bag is still upstairs?"

"I didn't notice that." She crossed her arms over the T-shirt she wore. It was her only attire. Her bare legs pressed together against the chill, toes curling into the floor. It took everything in him not to attack her on the kitchen table. "I heard the cab honk, then the front door.

I looked out to see you running out to it, wearing your jacket and—"

"You deduced the worst." She was never going to let him get away with a single thing. Privately that made him laugh, but he gave her his most aggrieved frown.

"Why didn't you wake me up if you wanted coffee?" she asked defensively.

"Sweetheart, I am many things, but stupid is not one of them. How many men get away with telling a woman to get up and make him coffee?"

"Fair point," she mumbled toward her toes.

"And I thought…" He ambled toward her, dropping the bag on the table before taking hold of her hips through the thin layer of cotton that barely covered them. "You would appreciate sleeping in, since I kept you up so late. And maybe you wouldn't wake up grouchy."

She diced him into little pieces with a glare.

He drew her closer, delicately crashing her against his growing arousal, liking the hitch of her breath. "And because I knew that once you were awake, I'd be hungry for more than an egg sandwich."

She ran her fingers over his collarbone and warmed the skin on his shoulders and upper arms with a soft exploration of her feminine hands. "You can always wake me for *that*," she assured him with a pouting moue that invited his kiss.

He brought her in tight now, enjoying the play of their bodies against one another as much as the play of the conversation. "I had something more important to do."

"Really?" Predictable frost entered her tone, making him chuckle. Her hands shifted to the middle of his chest, pressing.

"Yes," he confirmed, resurrecting his most bored and arrogant tone, purely for impact. "Among other things, I spent the morning redirecting my new staff to look for a property here in Montreal and see what is involved in drawing up incorporation documents for Canada instead of New York."

Her arms went limp. Her expression was dumbfounded. "Are you serious?"

"As a heart attack, baby." He surprised her with a dive to scoop her legs out from under her, giving her a little toss that made her scream before he caught her in the cradle of his arms and started for the stairs. "So don't ever doubt me again."

Natalie was suitably chastised for the rest of the day, cooking him a late breakfast, then suggesting some neighborhoods for his new offices. Maybe it was only something he was considering, but they wound up driving around the city in her car, scouting different blocks, then eating at a pub before going back to her place for a glass of wine, a movie and more incredible lovemaking.

She didn't allow herself any doubts until Sunday, after he'd woken her with a light tease of his tongue on her nipple, which led to lusty groans of ecstasy shortly thereafter. It was well into late morning and they were still dozing off their lovemaking, negotiating who would rise and make coffee, when he asked her what she wanted to do with the day.

"I have to pick up Zoey," she mumbled into her pillow. It had been hovering in her subconscious, waiting for the opportunity to be mentioned.

"From where?"

"Her grandmother's. It's a couple of hours out of the city." She lifted her head to see he wore his most neutral, arrested look, reserving his thoughts. "Heath is supposed to bring her back by supper, but he's always late. If I want her in bed at a reasonable hour on a school night, I have to get her myself." She looked toward the window, pleased to see streaks of sunlight behind the blinds, but sad to cut short their weekend. "It's not a bad drive on a nice day. I'll probably stay for coffee."

"With Heath? I'll drive," he stated before she could answer.

Jealous? She shunted off that thought, not wanting to build up his feelings into more than they really were.

"With his mother," she clarified. "Heath will be ice fishing up on the lake, which is why he gets Zoey home so late."

"I still want to drive." He swung his legs to the edge of the bed and rose. The cheeks of his butt were taut and firm. The muscles in his back flexed as he rolled his shoulders.

"Demitri…" She sat up.

"It's time for me to meet her, Nat." He glanced back at her, the implacability in his features not allowing for refusal. "Especially if we're all going to New York next weekend."

About that, she wanted to say, but he disappeared into the shower and didn't give her a chance to talk to him before they were in the car heading out of the city. By then she had gone around and through every avenue of thought on whether her behavior was wise. She kept coming back to his calling them a serious couple. He was considering working out of Montreal. If she didn't want to be with him, she should tell him to get out of her life right now, before he made big changes to his own.

She wanted to be with him.

She just wasn't convinced he would want to be with her *and* Zoey.

Despite Theo's comment still rubbing like sandpaper on his ego, Demitri knew he wasn't *really* like their father. The few times he'd had physical altercations had been with fully grown men who were drunk and trying to kill each other. He stopped violence, didn't perpetuate it.

As for relating to kids, okay, he didn't have the first idea, but Natalie was a two-for-one package, so he was going to have to figure it out. The one thing he couldn't be was too self-centered and inflexible to try. He really would be his father if he couldn't live with a child who didn't carry his own DNA.

Still, as casual and confident as he tried to appear about the whole thing, Natalie must have sensed his tension because she was very quiet on the drive, only speaking to point out a landmark or give him directions.

It was pretty countryside with rolling hills and churches nestled back in the trees and icicles hanging in claws from rocky escarpments. He could see why she was willing to let her daughter get away into this kind of fresh air and natural surroundings.

They arrived at a farmhouse where an older woman swept blown snow off the porch and Zoey threw a stick for a midsize mutt in the trampled snow.

Natalie introduced him to Claudette, who said she'd go in to put on fresh coffee, then she introduced him to Zoey, whose hair was covered with a crooked hat that Natalie called a toque when she straightened it.

"Grandma was going to take me to the barn to see the kittens. Do you like kittens?" Zoey asked, leaning way back to see his face.

"Who doesn't?" he asked, wondering if that was too glib. Frivolous banter was his fallback, but maybe you took a kid more seriously.

"Uncle Frank," she answered innocently. "They make him sneeze. C'mon. There's five. Like me."

"There's five of her?" Demitri mused to Natalie as they followed.

"You'll start to think so," she assured him, slanting a look up at him that told him she was reserving judgment, but watching closely.

He refused to be daunted. Surely Zoey couldn't be harder to schmooze than the average sociopathic celebrity demanding VIP treatment.

She wasn't. It turned out fine. Better than fine. They wandered the farm with her for almost an hour, admired the snowman she'd made with her cousins, located all the kittens in the barn and learned their names, waited while she gathered eggs and listened attentively when she explained each step of how her grandmother had turned the alpaca's fur into the matching hat and sweater she wore.

"You're being very patient," Natalie commented as they followed Zoey to the house.

He was startled by the remark, since he had yet to reach for any patience. He was here to meet the girl and he'd been getting to know what made her tick. She was five. He didn't expect her to discuss the day's stock-market numbers. She knew more about fish and hockey than a lot of the blowhards he'd met over the years and either laughed at his jokes or didn't get it and said something bemusing, which made him chuckle.

"I'm waiting for the hard part to start," he responded, indicating his watch. "It's been forty minutes and she hasn't asked for drugs, thrown a television off a balcony or gone viral on the internet with a nude selfie."

She snickered. "And that was just the one teen pop star?"

"Everyone always thought I was partying with them. I was trying to keep the lawsuits to a minimum."

They stayed for coffee and it was relaxed and easy. Claudette was one of those earth-mother sorts who made him feel at home immediately, not asking nosy questions or seeming overly curious about his relationship with Natalie. She projected warm acceptance, and he could see why Natalie treasured her.

Zoey colored at the table between him and Natalie as

the grown-ups talked, at one point asking, "Mom, do you want to help me?"

Demitri gave in to temptation and picked up a crayon. He hadn't messed around with them in years and the smell took him back to his own childhood, when Adara had tried to keep him quiet with drawing projects. He was missing work, he realized. There had been a part of him holding his breath as he and Natalie had looked at properties yesterday. Zoey had been the unknown quantity, but now he was beginning to see her as part of the broader picture, and felt more certainty he was making the right choice.

"Is that me?" Zoey asked, pausing her own coloring to watch.

He was showing off, sketching Zoey in primary colors. It was a shameless bid to win her affection, but where he thought the endgame was winning Natalie's, he found himself inordinately pleased by Zoey's "That's one for the fridge!"

Later that night, when Natalie showed him to the door, shadows edged her gaze as she asked a very weighty "Well?"

"Well, what?" he asked, deliberately obtuse. "Am I resentful that I'm being kicked out to a hotel? Just disappointed. I said I'd respect your boundaries where she's concerned and I will."

"That's not what I meant."

"I know what you meant." He stole a light kiss. "I'll be back tomorrow."

CHAPTER NINE

Going to New York was a step back into the fantasy world of Paris, which scared her. And she really should have seen the signs.

"Which one?" she'd asked, holding up two dresses from her closet. One was a very sophisticated blue cocktail dress she'd bought at a consignment store. The other was the black dress she'd worn on their first date.

"You're adorable," he'd replied with a shake of his head, going back to the travel arrangements he'd been making on his tablet. "I'll buy you something in New York," he had added in an aside.

"We could have shopped last weekend," she'd protested, but began to understand why even Montreal's excellent shopping wasn't good enough for him after he'd flown them in a chartered plane to New York and had shown them into his screamingly sophisticated penthouse.

How had she forgotten how rich he was?

They had spent the week having Parisian trysts in the afternoons before Zoey came home from school, then Natalie had cooked dinner for all of them. After a lifetime of catering to spoiled guests, one decently disciplined five-year-old was a piece of cake for Demitri. Zoey was quickly becoming one more female caught in the net of his effortless charisma. And so was Natalie, because he spent time on Zoey, not money, listening to her stories about school friends and playing games with her after her bath. The evenings had been domestic and nice.

And somehow Natalie had forgotten that even though Demitri might not have a real job at the moment, his family owned a worldwide chain of five-star hotels. He had a trust fund, an investment broker he talked to a few times a week and one of those credit cards without a limit. Also a top-floor apartment bigger than her house. With a pool.

"That's a lot of windows," Zoey had said when they'd entered his home, craning her neck up the twenty feet of panes that made Demitri's flat seem as if it occupied a place among the constellations. "You have a lot of books, too."

"I do," he'd agreed. "I've even read most of them, which I imagine surprises your mother. Have a look around. Don't go outside without me, though."

Zoey had run off to explore, but Natalie hadn't needed to catalogue the professional decor or the signatures on the paintings or eyeball the view from the terrace. She'd already been suffering a fresh set of panic as she had seen a brand-new reason his family might have no desire to see her at their little dinner. Peasant stock did not belong here.

Except it wasn't just a little dinner, she found out over breakfast.

Eggs benedict, strawberry waffles and pastries had magically appeared while she'd been trying to figure out Demitri's espresso machine. Zoey thought it was Christmas when the whipping cream came out of the delivery bin.

"How do you feel about dinosaurs, Zoey? I thought we'd visit the Natural History Museum today," Demitri said when they sat down to eat.

"Oh, that sounds fun," Natalie enthused. "I've always wanted to go there."

"I'm afraid I'll have to take you another time." He

stabbed a hash brown off her plate. "You have an appointment at the spa."

"Do I?" she said, lifting her chin in dismay.

"You're also meeting with a stylist."

"Is there something wrong with the way I look?"

"Not at all. Wear what you like. But I'll be in a tuxedo and all the other women will be in gowns. I thought you would prefer one."

"All— As in lots of women? I thought this was family dinner?"

"It's a white-tie ball," he said, as if she ought to have known. As if those happened in the normal world.

"For how many?" she exclaimed.

"Two hundred couples or so. You didn't ask," he protested at her glare. "It's not a secret. It's a charity thing for the homeless. Adara does it every year. Look it up."

"And Zoey is invited to this thing?"

"Zoey will meet my niece and nephews this evening along with their nannies, all bonded and vetted and valued for their attentiveness to the children. They'll only be a few floors away at the hotel, should anyone feel a need to check in." His tone said that he expected Natalie to suffer the separation anxiety, not Zoey. "Apparently Evie enjoys playing with her boy cousins, but would love to spend time with a little girl." To Zoey, he added, "Evie is three and likes princesses, too."

Demitri must have a secret fetish for them himself. An hour later, Natalie began receiving the royal treatment, from a mud wrap to a Swedish massage to drinking a mimosa during her pedicure. She couldn't remember a time she'd felt so pampered and renewed. All of her skin was waxed and lotioned, detoxified and revitalized. The stylist met with her twice before she dressed, taking measurements and consulting with the salon, agreeing with the plan to weave a sparkling ribbon into her updo so her hair became a subtle crown. Her makeup was a masterful understatement highlighting all of her best features, and finally, the dress…

Natalie hadn't worn a long gown since high school graduation, and that one had been a thrift store find in garish pink with puffy sleeves.

Demitri had much better taste. According to the stylist, he'd chosen her gown himself. Nothing so predictable as burgundy for winter, it was a shade between lavender and gray, the color muted by the crushed velvet fabric, but it made her eyes look like mysterious pools in the Scottish highlands. Strapless, with intricate detailing at her hip that gathered the skirt before allowing it to flare around her shoes, the confection clung to her curves to make the most of her silhouette. A matching jacket that really only covered her shoulders and upper arms ensured she wouldn't freeze to death.

Her shoes added height—a lot of height. They were deceptively simple black things, but the underside matched the color of her dress and the tops, open toe but closed back, drew a sparkling line from the ankle strap down one side of her foot and across her toes. More important, they looked as if they'd kill her yet made her feel as though she walked on clouds. She could dance all night.

She couldn't accept this, she kept thinking, reminding herself he would have done this for countless women before her. It still felt as though she was climbing too high, starting to feel special and treasured.

"The jewelry is on loan," the stylist said, trying a few different pieces before settling on an antique cameo on a thick silver rope chain and a pair of sapphire studs. "But I've done this for other clients and if I get it right…" She debated a bracelet, then rejected it. "The gentleman will buy them for you."

"Oh, I don't expect anything."

The stylist smiled with smooth acceptance of what she plainly thought was a lie. "Of course not."

Natalie found herself acknowledging it was a lie. Not the part about expecting jewelry, but the part about not expecting *anything*. She was starting to dream of things she had cautioned herself never to expect. Never to *want*.

Love. Family. Commitment. Marriage.

A life partner. Another baby.

Because she was falling in love with Demitri. Deeply and irrevocably.

Demitri might have spent the day brooding about the coming meeting with his family tonight if his mind hadn't been completely occupied trying to keep up with a five-year-old in a museum. And the Empire State Building. And a world-famous toy store. After feeding ducks in the park, he finally brought Zoey back to watch a movie on his flat screen, set a bowl of popcorn in her lap and went to shave and change.

When he heard the door and Zoey's gasp of "Mommy!" he smiled at the bittersweet sound. Bitter because time was running out—he would be facing his siblings soon—but sweet because Zoey's wonder was so delightfully expressive.

There was something pure about her view of the world that dusted the cynicism out of his own eyes. She had no reason to hide enthusiasm or curiosity or any emotion. She'd never been bruised by life, let alone deeply hurt by it. He found himself wanting to protect and preserve her innocent confidence in adults. Where anger and resentment had made him see his siblings as deluded in their joy of being with their children, he felt privileged that Natalie was sharing her daughter with him. He wanted to guard her, spend time with her and watch her flourish into the bright, funny, self-possessed woman she was meant to become.

The more time he spent with the two of them, the more certain he was that he wanted to come home to them every day. Which flummoxed him. He'd never seen himself married with a ready-made family.

Natalie would never see him in the role, either, if he quit on his family because things had turned hard. That made the stakes on tonight's reconciliation higher than anything he'd ever undertaken.

It was an unnerving state to be in, one he brushed away as determinedly as he smoothed his bow tie. Shrugging into his jacket, he walked out to the living, room where he took a punch to the heart. It was a ground-shaking reaction, considering he was a connoisseur of beautiful women.

But she was *so* beautiful. The color of the gown had caught his eye, making him think of chain mail and strength and Saint Jeanne d'Arc, while still reflecting the softness and light of Natalie's true nature. It enhanced her beauty, rather than outshining it, so the impact was the woman, not the dress. Curvy and desirable, but elegant and resilient and completely feminine.

She stole his breath.

And her laughter at her daughter's excitement, joyful and teasing and so loving, turned up the piece of himself that he'd buried long ago, exposing it to the sun so it burned and shook.

Natalie caught sight of him and straightened, mouth forming a pretty "Oh" that he wanted to kiss.

"I thought I was overdressed, but…" She swallowed, blushing a little while her gaze traveled over him like soft, feminine fingertips, touching all the places that responded most acutely to her every caress. "You look very handsome."

"You look perfect," he assured her, crossing to graze his lips against her cheekbone, lingering to take in the feminine scents designed to disorient a man. "Mesmerizing."

Natalie blushed again and ducked her head to ask Zoey to take their photo. The little girl was beside herself with admiration for the two of them, and then quivered with excitement at riding in the limo.

Demitri took them into the underground parking lot beneath the Makricosta Manhattan rather than having them dropped at the front doors. As they arrived, he made the call to his sister-in-law to have the VIP elevator opened. Demitri had figured there was only one person with enough clout to get them into the hotel without notice while remaining secure enough to know she'd be forgiven for interfering: Nic's wife, Rowan. She'd become Adara's best friend and she was also booking all the entertainment for this event, so one more group in the elevator wasn't suspicious.

This particular elevator was typically used to smuggle in celebrities trying to avoid detection by the paparazzi. They stepped directly into it from the car.

When they arrived on the penthouse floor, the door of the end one swung open before they reached it.

Nic. Damn. Demitri had asked Rowan to hang back and take them down to the party herself without mentioning to any of his siblings his intention to attend.

Looking rather like a vengeful god, Nic sent a level stare at Demitri that hit like a punch in the face. His features were oddly familiar, Theo-like yet older, with a Nordic cast to his cheekbones and blond hair.

"Your wife is expecting us," Demitri said, falling back on a well-used, affable expression of indifference.

"So she has just informed me." Judging by his tone, Nic didn't appreciate Demitri going behind his back in talking to her.

"I waited until Theo and Jaya had dropped off Zephyr and left," Rowan said in her welcoming Irish accent, smiling as she came forward from behind him. "But I don't keep things from Nic. Please come in."

Despite being famous from childhood, Rowan was always pleasantly self-effacing. Tonight she was as attractive as she always looked on-screen, wearing a gown that clung like emerald paint to her flawless figure, black hair loose and straight. Her smile seemed natural, but she *was* an actress. She had sounded eager to assist when he first contacted her, but now Demitri wasn't sure about her, given that she'd revealed his presence here to Nic.

"You must be Natalie. And Zoey," she greeted warmly.

Natalie seemed caught between intimidation and sensitivity to the undercurrents. Glancing at Demitri, she said, "I don't want to impose if we weren't expected."

Nic turned his sharp gaze on her, blinking as though he was taking a photograph. "It's fine."

Natalie might have relaxed if he'd smiled, but he didn't.

He only added, "I'll fetch Evie," and disappeared down a hall.

"We don't know much about the falling-out," Rowan said delicately. "But Nic and I are happy to help mend fences."

Were they? She really was a hell of an actress, managing to look and sound sincere when it was obvious Nic was the furthest thing from happy.

Natalie kept her eyes downcast, but Demitri was so attuned to her, he could hear her silent screams for him to get them the hell out of here.

Excellent job of showing her how well he integrated with his family.

"Look, Rowan, if—" he started, but was interrupted by Nic's return.

The ferocious bear had turned into a house pet while he was gone, judging from the doting tone of his voice as he carried his daughter into the lounge. "I want you to meet someone," he told the petite girl wearing a stained T-shirt and turned up jeans over bare toes.

Demitri really looked at the girl for once. Not the obvious details like her dark hair and Asian features—she had been adopted from one of the war-torn countries Nic used to report on when he'd been a feet-on-the-ground journalist. No, Demitri looked at the protective way Nic held her. The connection between them, demonstrated by the way Evie's arm curled around his neck and she gazed at him with utter trust.

If a hard case like this man could become a caring father to a child who'd had a rough start, surely there was hope for himself with Zoey?

"Who is it?" Evie asked, letting her gaze swing out to hit each of the adults, then tilt and fix on Zoey.

"Her name is Zoey. Uncle Demitri brought her to visit. Will you say hello?" He squatted so the girls were eye to eye.

"'Lo," Evie murmured, pushing a finger into her shy smile. She took it out to point down the hall, then mentioned her cousin, Theo's boy. "Zephyr's nanny brought face paints. I'm gonna be a cat. What do you like to be?"

Zoey looked up at Natalie, eager as a retriever. "Can I be a butterfly?"

Natalie hesitated, thick lashes sweeping up like a scimitar to shave Demitri's cheek, her flick of a smile telegraphing, *If only adult interactions were so simple*.

"Let's ask the nanny," Natalie said to Zoey, urging Evie to show them the way. "I'll give her my number so she can phone me if you need me."

Moments later, they reached the ballroom floor and exited the silent elevator behind Nic and Rowan. Demitri held back with Natalie, saying, "I'm sorry that was so…"

"Awkward?" Natalie prompted ruefully. "It's fine. He probably doesn't like secrets any more than you do."

Demitri hadn't thought of his request to Rowan as anything but trying to avoid pitting Nic against Theo and Adara on his behalf. Family relationships were bloody complicated.

Gripping Natalie's hand in his, palm to palm, Demitri drew her to the entrance to the ballroom, where a full concert band played over the din of conversation.

Security stopped him at the door.

"They're with us," Nic said.

"I still have to report that you're here," the tuxedoed man said to Demitri, making clear exactly how wide the chasm was between him and his siblings.

"I'll report myself," he said, impatience edging into his tone. He tugged Natalie along behind him, into the throng.

They turned heads. Not just because he was moving so determinedly through the crowd, either. People recognized him. The explanations for his abrupt departure from the company would have made the gossip rounds in many forms, he was sure.

The startled reactions worked in his favor, however. Once people noted he was here, they craned their necks to catch the reaction of the host and hostess. It pointed him like a compass to the small knot of people opposite the banquet table.

Gideon saw him first, narrowing a piercing, hostile glare on him even as a minion slid in close to whisper in his ear.

"I can see that," Gideon mouthed.

Demitri knew the moment Gideon identified his date. His demeanor changed from outright aggression to caution. He reached to his wife, getting her attention, excusing them from the group to step away and await them.

Adara looked up, started with recognition and then her posture softened in welcome.

Natalie tried to work her hand from his, and Demitri

realized he was crushing her fine bones. He softened his hold but kept her hand, linking their fingers, recognizing that he'd always flaunted brassy, interchangeable women at these occasions to shield himself from deeper emotions.

Real emotions.

Natalie was a white flag. Bringing her was a statement that he cared about her. He was unarmed. Vulnerable.

It wasn't a comfortable state. It was terrifying. If they rejected him, if they rejected *them*, he didn't know what he'd do.

The minute he was in earshot of his sister, he said, "You didn't deserve the way I treated you. I'm sorry." Old pain threatened to catch up with him as so much of what he'd faced with Natalie's help confronted him in the shadowed gaze of his sister.

Natalie's hand stopped squirming in his, and her other one covered the back of his, sandwiching him in subtle reassurance. Giving him the strength to finish.

"I just wanted to wish you a happy birthday, Adara." He reached forward with his free arm to catch his sister around the shoulders and draw her in, feeling her jerk in surprise that he would hug her, not having done so since they were both children. "If you'd rather I left, I will."

"Of course I want you here," she said after a stunned moment of surprise. Her arms went around him, hugging hard. She added shakily, "I'm so happy to see you, I'm going to cry."

"We can't have that," he scoffed, drawing back, moved that she'd forgiven him so easily. *Family.* It really was a luxury not to be taken for granted. He clawed for lazy humor so emotion wouldn't overwhelm him. "Your husband already wants to kill me for upsetting you. I'll write a suitably remorseful check to the shelter. Will that make you smile?"

Adara laughed and swept fingertips under her eyes.

Gideon's expression mellowed, then flicked to Natalie and came back with one brow raised in question at Demitri. *What are your intentions there*? he seemed to ask.

"It's nice to see you again, Natalie," Adara said, pulling herself together to demonstrate her perfect manners.

Natalie's covering fingers fell away from Demitri's and her other hand went limp in his. She lifted a brave but pained smile to her hosts. "I'm glad to be here. I wanted to take this chance to—"

"Do *not* apologize," Demitri warned her.

She flashed him a look of ire. "I can if I want."

"That's not why I brought you. And you know it," he told her in a growl. They'd shared so much, become so much, it would insult both of them if she made apologies for how they'd come together.

"Humph," she snorted, eyeing her fresh manicure of peach paint and glittering gold tips. "All those times you told me you weren't the boss of me, turns out you think you are."

"Really?" he challenged. "Take the blame, then. She cold-bloodedly seduced me for the sole purpose of destroying my career and hurting our family," he said offhandedly.

"No, I—" She frowned crossly at him, but before she could clarify, he continued.

"I have to fix this one, Natalie. *I* have to." It sucked. Royally. He hated it. But he was going to do it. She had to see that he was willing to go the distance.

"He's used to being the one at fault, Natalie," Gideon said, humor smooth and dry as always. "Let him have this."

"Thanks," Demitri muttered at his brother-in-law, finding the remark oddly heartening. Gideon wouldn't be making light if he still wanted to kill him.

"Theo has seen you. Were you going to speak to him?" Adara asked with a pull of concern between her brows.

"Yes," Demitri said firmly, setting a decisive hand on Natalie's back to turn her toward his brother. "But we'll come back. I want your opinion on my new venture," he told Gideon, genuinely respectful of the man's business acuity.

As they approached Theo and his wife, Jaya stepped forward to greet Natalie warmly. Jaya wore a lemon-yellow sari and her exotic looks were amplified by her husband's flawless, ironed straight tuxedo.

"I've been anxious for a debriefing about the work in France," Jaya said to Natalie. "We always promise we won't talk shop at these things, but five minutes, Theo? Please? Can I be horribly clichéd and ask you to come to the ladies' room with me while we talk, Natalie? I feel like I'm risking a wardrobe malfunction. I need to retuck."

"Your wife has never liked me," Demitri told Theo as Jaya made off with his moral support. It was probably for the best. Adara was soft and naturally forgiving. Theo's kinship would not be so easy to regain. He didn't relish Natalie watching him crash and burn.

But some said emulation was the sincerest form of flattery and Demitri wanted to emulate Theo. He would never be perfect the way Theo was, but somehow his withdrawn, reclusive brother had earned the devotion of a sweet, loving woman. Demitri needed to know how that was done.

"I've never liked you, either, if you want the truth," Theo remarked as the women disappeared.

"Is that the best you can do?" Demitri scoffed with a fake husk of a laugh, pretending the lazy blow hadn't landed hard enough to leave a mark.

"No," Theo said flatly.

Demitri rocked back on his heels, nodding as the silence stretched. "No, you can refuse to talk to me at all. It's a brutally effective punishment, Theo. I don't have a spare in Nic the way you do. Gideon can't stand me. You're all I've got for a brother."

Theo didn't look at him. He'd gone very still. Slowly he took a sip of the soda he held. "Gideon runs a tight ship. He doesn't put up with jackassery of any kind. I never make mistakes, so he doesn't have anything to call me up for. You've made yourself a pet project for him, though. That's the only reason he rides you."

Theo was letting a few emotions creep into the conversation—annoying ones like superiority and weary exasperation. It was his version of warming up. Demitri took heart.

"And Nic—" Theo began, but Demitri stopped him.

"I know. You would have talked about him if you could have. Frankly, I'm glad that you have at least one good memory from our childhood," he said sincerely, unable to suppress the deep anguish anymore, aware it flashed into his expression before he was able to control his emotions outwardly even if they threatened to overwhelm him internally.

Theo acknowledged the statement with a lowering of his brows and tightening of his lips.

"I shouldn't have said what I did," Demitri added, guts clawing with shame. "I don't expect you to forgive me, but I am sorry."

Nothing for a long moment, then, "Those things weren't your fault. I shouldn't have made out as if they were. We were kids. None of that was our fault. And you're not like him. *I* shouldn't have said *that*."

Their gazes met for a fraction of a heartbeat, just long enough to see the shattered emotion in the other and look away to hide their own.

A weird relief weakened Demitri's limbs. He'd needed to hear it. It allowed him to believe he might be good enough for Natalie after all.

"For what it's worth," Theo continued drily, "Nic has himself so together he makes me feel like the idiotic younger brother. So you'll always have a place in my life."

"Good to know," Demitri said with a catch of laughter, pleased to be back on trashing terms with Theo. "By the way, you don't pay Natalie enough. I'll be stealing her for the firm I'm starting."

"Is that what you're doing with her?" Theo asked, giving him a sharp look.

"No," Demitri said in a rare moment of complete sincerity. "I'm going to ask her to marry me." It made him proud to say it, and he liked the way Theo absorbed the news with a thoughtful, approving nod.

"Good luck." He even sounded like he meant it.

Natalie dropped her lipstick into her pocketbook and met Jaya's gaze in the mirror. "That's ten minutes. Have we given them enough time?"

Jaya's painted smile twitched. "Was I that obvious? I really have been wanting your impressions on how the new software was received."

Natalie shrugged, not feeling she'd told Jaya anything she wouldn't have heard through other channels, but the topic had been a nice path around the scandal that had arisen from Natalie's assignment in France.

"I think we were right to let them duke it out in private," Natalie said, referring to Demitri and Theo. "I just hope they have. Family isn't something you can have so much of that you can afford to throw any of it away."

"That's what I kept telling Theo after he ignored Demitri's call!" As they walked back, Jaya told her about a disagreement in her own family involving her cousin. It had gone on for years, breaking many hearts. She was so engaging, Natalie started when someone touched her arm.

It was Rowan. She waved them into conversation with

her and Gideon, leaning gleefully toward Jaya as she gave a little nod to something across the room. "Don't look now, but the planets have aligned."

Natalie followed their gazes to all four siblings standing in a group, talking animatedly.

"Oh," Jaya sighed, setting a hand over her heart. "I was starting to worry it would never happen."

"This will mean the world to Nic," Rowan murmured with a poignant creak in her tone.

"And Adara," Gideon said.

Demitri had needed this, too. Natalie felt a wistful pride in being part of making it happen. For a moment, she even felt equal to these other partners in this mystic circle, gazing with happiness for the group of laughing adults who hadn't known joy as children.

Not long after, they toasted Adara with champagne and sang along when Adara's favorite chart-topping crooner led the crowd in "Happy Birthday." Then the dancing started.

"Evie wants Zoey to spend the night," Rowan found Natalie to say. "Would you mind? She'll be heartbroken if Zoey leaves. One of us will have to go up to her."

Rowan had booked several rooms for the musicians she'd hired to entertain the crowd, but one of those suites had been set aside for Natalie and Demitri. If Zoey needed her mother in the night, they'd only be a few doors away. Natalie made the call to Zoey and had to pull the phone away from her ear when her daughter squealed, "She said yes!"

The enchantment of the evening deepened as Natalie absorbed that she would be making love with Demitri tonight. Resting her head on his shoulder, she surrendered to the sexual pull he always exerted over her. Her jacket was off and his lips touched her bare shoulder. Male fingertips caressed up her arm. She lightly traced the hollow at the back of his neck.

This was so perfect. So loving.

Holding eye contact with him was always a stumble into sexual heat. Tonight it was a blind gallop into a conflagration. He was so handsome, carefree in an authentic way that hurt to look at. Every point where she came in contact with him stung with need, tightening her airway and wetting her eyes at the magnitude of the moment.

She loved him so much.

"We have a room," she reminded in a voice husked with growing passion.

"Do you want to leave?" He searched her gaze, the delving deep enough to make her insides shake.

She nodded, ducking her head to hide her reaction, tracing a hand beneath his open coat across the tensed muscles of his waist.

The crowd had thinned. Nic and Rowan had already left, since they had to be up with the children in the morning. Adara hugged them and Gideon bussed Natalie's cheek with a kiss, sounding sincere when he said, "Thank you for coming."

She and Demitri walked out hand in hand, sexual tension climbing between them with each step. When they entered the suite, he threw the entry card on the table and said, "Come here, beautiful."

She spun into his arms, crashing herself against him so he grunted at the hit and wrapped her arms around his neck in abandoned joy. His mouth was everything she'd been waiting for, his hair spiky between her fingers, his body already aroused and thick against her—

"Easy, Natalie," he soothed in a masterful voice, arms hardening to still her from wriggling through his skin to adhere to his bones. His nose grazed her cheekbone; his brow touched hers. "We have time. Lots of time."

A lifetime? It wasn't like her to believe in permanence, but for once she let herself trust he would always be here for her.

And he wouldn't be rushed when it came to getting what he wanted from her. He *would* seduce her, holding her pinned to his steely body while he drew out his long, lazy kisses that thoroughly plundered her mouth.

She couldn't move in his hold, could only tell him with her lips and tongue and a ragged, lusty moan that he was torturing her. Her blood pounded her arteries in painful hammer blows of need. His heart slammed behind his chest wall, reverberating against her resting palm, the only evidence he matched her excitement.

That and their breaths mingling in shaken hisses.

"I want you so much," she whispered when he nipped at the straining cord along the side of her neck, then closed her eyes, abandoning herself to his caresses.

"This is all I've been thinking about since I first saw you tonight. Your skin. Your laugh. The way you catch your breath."

She did it now as he tilted her hips into his, sex to sex, need to need.

Stropping her face against his spicy-smelling neck, she said, "I want to be naked. I want to feel you."

"Yes." The word hissed out of him and he stepped back to turn her, lowering her zipper down her spine with sensual care, forehead tilted against her crown. His soft laughter pooled hotly against the back of her bare neck. "These dimples are my fatal weakness, Natalie," he said as her gown slid to the floor. He set two thumbs against the upper swells of her bottom, where the high cut of her French lingerie framed them. "After Lyon, I agonized that I would never see them again."

She smiled, made joyous by the confession.

His fingers moved into her hair, gently pulling pins and

dropping them. The quiet attentiveness, the tenderness of his touch, the graze of his clothing against her bare skin made it the most romantic moment of her life. She felt like a bride. Cherished. Loved.

Tonight she would let herself believe that she was. Somehow she was more than all the other women he'd been with combined.

Her own movements slowed as she grew determined to savor. Remember each touch. Each breath.

When he turned her, he grazed the backs of his fingers along the side of her breast. Leaned in to kiss her sweetly. "You're so beautiful, Natalie."

She believed him and undressed him between kisses, pushing his jacket off his shoulders, pulling away his bow tie, opening the buttons hidden in the ruffles of his shirt. When she got to his fly, he reached into his pocket to remove a strip of three condoms.

"Always prepared," she teased, pushing his pants down his hips.

"Wishful thinking that came true," he said, caressing her jaw and rueful smile. "I thought you'd be sleeping with Zoey tonight."

Kicking free of the last of his clothes, he set his feet apart and drew her into his nude body, making them both release shattered breaths at the contact of skin on skin. His fingers tangled in her panties and slid them down, urging her to leave them on the floor as he drew her to the bedroom.

The unhurried purity of the moment encased her in a glow, walking like the only two humans on earth to the bed. Her heart was wide-open to him, taking in his reverent study of her form as though it was a vow. She would never love anyone the way she loved him, she realized. Tears stung the backs of her eyes. Her feelings went beyond his primitive sexuality and masculine beauty. The fighter in her rested when he was near. Surrendered and trusted.

As he pressed her to her back on the soft mattress, parted her legs and entered her with his strength, she clenched her eyes against brimming wetness.

"Look at me, Natalie."

"I can't," she whispered. "It's too much."

"I've got you. I'm going to take care of you."

He would, she saw, when she dared to open her eyes. His dark eyes were deeply colored with sincerity. His muscles quivered as he held back. Always so generous, especially in bed.

She twisted, agonized by the acute intimacy and pleasure-pain of holding him within her, with the difficulty of stifling the words in her throat.

"You're holding back," he accused, thrusting with care to draw out each sensation. "Why? Give me all of you. Everything," he commanded.

She couldn't keep it in. She let go, moaning, "I love you. I love you." She shuddered as she released all her defenses, poured her love over him and prayed she'd get a piece of him in return.

CHAPTER TEN

DEMITRI HAD KNOWN tonight would be good. Sex with Natalie was easily the best he'd ever had. In those first days after their split in France, he'd told himself their lovemaking had merely benefited from the build of knowledge between them, as it typically could when affairs were drawn out. They'd learned how to tantalize the other to the limits of their sanity and enjoyed every second of it.

But here he was, missionary, barely having kissed her before he'd been inside her, and rather than emptying him, she had filled him. He was better than satisfied. He was moved—by words that she'd told him didn't mean anything.

He had little trust in the phrase himself. He'd heard it dozens of times from women in the throes of passion. He would have dismissed her saying it, but he couldn't. He wanted it to be true. He wanted to believe they really had been making love every time he'd touched her, building toward this moment, this emotion.

Because he was in it. In love.

It was the only explanation for his utter transformation. She wasn't changing him. He was changing himself for her, because she deserved better than he'd been.

He loved her.

Gently drawing away, he adjusted them, then gathered her against where his heart was only now easing to a resting pace. He'd never felt so fragile in his life. It was terrifying. Completely unfamiliar.

He wasn't an emotionally dependent man. He was connected to his siblings, their opinion mattered to him, and when he'd finally pushed them away to the point that they'd ostracized him, he'd quietly agonized.

But this, with Natalie, was so much more. From the moment he'd decided to find her—before that, even—he had been looking for ways not just to maintain their connection, but intertwine them. Knot her to him indelibly.

He wanted to tell her how much she meant to him, but he remembered so clearly her disparagement of her ex. It would gut him right now if she brushed off his saying something he'd felt, let alone expressed aloud. If he wound up pushing her away with those words, he'd be devastated. But he still needed her to realize how far she'd brought him from what he'd been.

"Thank you for coming with me tonight, Natalie. I couldn't have made peace with my family without you."

She drew her arm off him and reached for the sheet. He pulled it around her and snugged her into his front more firmly, running a hand up and down her back, absently encouraging her to melt into him again, thoughts still drifting in a thousand directions as he tried to take in all the ways she'd enriched his life.

He tried to work up how to propose without risking his soul.

"All those times Adara nagged me about these little reunions, I couldn't see myself being a part of it. Now the pieces are falling into place." He should have stopped there, he would think later, but the next words came out of his mouth. "Should we get married? So it's not so confusing for Zoey? I'd like to be in your bed every night, you know."

Natalie shimmied away from the heavy weight of his arms, heart pared like an apple. For a moment all her brain could conjure was panicked expletives. He wasn't acknowledging her expression of love. He was saying thank-you, as though she'd brought him a fresh cup of coffee.

And starting to enlighten her as to why he'd brought her here: so he fit in with the siblings who had spouses and children. While she'd been falling in love, he'd been repackaging himself as a family man to find acceptance with his siblings. She didn't blame him. She was totally sincere in wanting him to strengthen his relationship with them on every level.

She just didn't understand why, *why* she had to be an instrument. A means to a prize rather than the prize itself. He'd told her last night that he was fixing his relationship with his family, but that had been a lie. Maybe just a fabrication. Maybe he didn't even see it, but she did. She always saw where her responsibility began and ended.

She wouldn't have been so hurt right now if he'd been honest with her about it up front. She probably wouldn't even have said no, because as he'd rightly pointed out, she was a soft touch, especially about things like family. If he'd told her this was why he'd needed her here, she would have found a way without letting her daughter attach to him and without giving up her heart to him.

But she couldn't do this for the rest of her life. She couldn't love him with all her heart and know he'd only married her for what she represented, not who she really was. She took on a lot for other people, but that was more responsibility than she was willing to carry. It wasn't fair to her and it would never be fair to Zoey.

"Demitri…" She swung legs that wouldn't hold her to the edge of the bed, then sat there, face covered. *Stupid, stupid Natalie.* Had she actually started to believe all the sparkle and glitter, laughter and lovemaking, added up to more than a nice chemical match with a very rich man?

"I know you don't want to get married," he said, coming up on an elbow behind her. "But for Zoey's sake—"

"For Zoey's sake I have to say no," she said, voice coarse. She stood, forcing her weak knees to lock, then searched out a hotel robe from the closet.

"Why?" The question was cold and hard.

"Because we'll end up divorced." She flung an exasperated hand into the air. "Listen, this is my fault. I started believing in the fantasy again. I know better than to imagine I'm ever going to get something real—"

"The fantasy," he interrupted, fairly spitting the word. "The one where you pretend you're one of those barfly tarts I used to pick up because acting like that is so much better than living your real life."

"Hey!" she cried, not liking how nasty this was getting.

"You don't like the way it sounds? Neither do I. You might have warned me that you were just enjoying the ride, Nat. Was saying you loved me part of the fantasy, too?"

So he *had* heard. And he was throwing it in her face. She jerked back as though it was a physical object striking her in the nose.

"Don't you dare act as if I'm the only one using someone!" She clenched her fists. "You only brought me here so you could look like the rest of them! I set my expectations very low. I've never had any other choice, but don't ask me to marry you just so you have a child to take to the family picnic."

"Because I'm that shallow," he said, throwing himself onto his feet, naked and furious, striding past her to walk out and find his pants in the lounge. Jamming his legs into them, he shouted, "You know what you want, Natalie? For me to be as self-involved and unreliable as your dad and your husband so you can tell yourself we're all alike and push us away. You can't count on others if you never *do*, you know. But you just love being responsible for everything, don't you? Well, good news, sweetheart. This one's all on you."

He slammed out of the suite.

Someone sat down beside him at the bar.

Nic.

Demitri silently swore. Things were just getting better and better.

Nic caught the bartender's eye and motioned to the drink in front of Demitri, indicating he wanted the same.

"Take mine. I don't want it," Demitri said, sliding it over a few inches. All his old coping strategies were shot and he hadn't found new ones beyond talking things out with Natalie, and he was so furious with her...

And so hurt...

End up divorced. Fantasy.

Nic didn't touch the drink. Didn't say anything. Only settled onto the stool, forearms on the bar, key card rotating on its edge between his fingers and thumb against the mahogany. His tuxedo jacket was gone along with his bow tie, his shirt untucked.

"Come to tell me you didn't like my talking to your wife behind your back?" Demitri guessed.

"No," Nic said with a measure of surprise, click-clicking the card against the glossed wood. "I didn't like it, but that's not why I'm here. Natalie called our suite. She wanted to come get Zoey— It's okay," he said at Demitri's curse, holding up a hand. "Ro talked her into letting the kids sleep till morning. She was inviting her over for a glass of wine when I left. I figured there weren't too many places a man goes when he's had it out with a woman. Found you on the first try."

"And why would you want to, Nic?" Demitri asked tiredly. It was late, Demitri was thinking. Far too late for this.

Nic pursed his mouth in thought, profile not unlike Theo's. Something in his features reminded Demitri of an old photo Adara had of their maternal grandfather. It was so odd. Made him feel less as though Nic was a complete stranger, even though he was.

"You didn't have to go behind my back, you know. You could have come to me," Nic said.

Demitri snorted, shook his head, baffled by the whole thing. He thought of Natalie telling him he had a right to his confusion and had to ask, "Why would I expect you to help me? Can I ask you something, Nic? And be honest. Do you remember me? Because I've got nothing."

Nic flinched, making Demitri feel as if he'd accidentally run over the guy's dog.

"Why would you remember me? You were a baby," Nic said, picking up the untouched drink and smelling it. Sipping once. "Yeah, I remember you. You liked to take your clothes off. Made us laugh."

Demitri choked on a chuckle. Couldn't help it. *True to form*, he thought, and immediately wanted to repeat the story to Natalie. It was the sort of thing that would make her laugh.

God, he loved her laugh. Loved her. *Hell.*

"Does Natalie know about any of that? What we came from?" Nic asked.

"She's the only one I've ever talked to about it." Something twisted in his chest, reaching out to her across the walls and floors, trying to get to her. He'd thought she understood him. Accepted him.

Nic's thumb worked the edge of the glass, nodded. "Yeah, it looked as if you two were pretty close. What happened?"

"Man, you really are an investigative journalist, aren't you?"

"Just trying to help," Nic said, turning his head and

looking disturbingly sincere. "She seems like a good person. I don't think you would have walked out on the family business over a woman you didn't love. Did you tell her?"

The word was like a knife to the heart. "She said it wasn't enough," he said, feeling the blade twist in his chest. He was a fantasy. Not real. A vehicle for pleasure, not a man of substance—exactly what he'd always portrayed himself as, so he probably deserved this heartbreak he was suffering, but he couldn't stand it. He didn't know how to live without her. Not anymore.

Nic swore under his breath. "She does not look like the kind of woman who would dice up a man when he laid it out like that."

As Nic's words penetrated, Demitri frowned. Eyed Nic. "No, that was something she said when she was talking about why she never wanted to remarry. I didn't actually tell her…"

He sounded like an idiot even to himself. He'd been so busy trying to protect himself, he'd left her hanging with her own declaration.

"I screwed up, didn't I?" For once not deliberately.

"Kinda sounds like it." Nic scratched under his chin. "Did you propose?"

Demitri winced. Longed for the days when he messed up and didn't care. Didn't feel it like broken glass coursing through his veins.

"Not with a ring. Not properly," he admitted.

A big breath expanded Nic's chest. He blew it out slowly. "I'm no advice columnist, but I've proofed a few," he said drily. "Here's the thing I do know. If you want to win a woman, you have to go all in. Give her everything you've got. Pride. Self-worth. Heart. Soul. All of it. Nothing held back."

"I wish it was that easy," Demitri said, thinking of how

hard it was to get Natalie to accept anything. That last accusation of his, about her always wanting to be responsible for everything, not counting on anyone, had been true. In his experience, women expected men's wallets to be opened on their behalf. He had never understood Natalie's deference and protests and putting of others first.

I set my expectations very low...

He'd heard that differently, thinking she was referring to him, too furious about the fantasy remark to process anything properly, but as he thought about why and how she'd become such a little soldier about responsibility, he saw a girl who'd been pressed into service and neglected in her own way. He wondered how many times she had wanted to go to the movies with friends, or continue her ice dancing, and her mother had had to say no. Not by choice, but because Natalie was needed. She didn't resent it, he knew, but life had cheated her so many times. Even her young-adult years of pursuing her education and making mistakes with boys had only lasted one night. Long enough to get pregnant, grow up and never do anything for herself again.

Except steal a few days in France. Other than that, she probably hadn't had a selfish moment in her life. Even her heart, her love, had been given away without her daring to ask for something in return.

Of course she loved him. Of course the words would mean something to her, if they were said with sincerity. The way she loved her daughter, her dead family, was fierce and enduring. She would love him, Demitri, until the end of time, and he was privileged, honored, to realize she'd come to feel such an emotion toward him.

"Thanks, Nic," he said, slapping his brother on the shoulder as he rose, hardened with purpose. "I know what to do." Throwing a few bills on the bar for the drink, he added, "Don't let her leave with Zoey before I get there."

* * *

Natalie wanted to shrink away and die, but Zoey had misplaced her bunny somewhere in Nic and Rowan's suite and refused to leave without it.

Rowan had urged Natalie to sleep on things last night, but when Natalie had dragged her sorry, unrested body out of bed, the suite had still been empty. Now she just wanted to collect her daughter and head back to Canada on whichever transport her credit card could afford.

But it wasn't happening.

And she was starting to see why Demitri found the Makricosta collective so annoying with their inclusive remarks and their cheery engagement with all the children. Everyone showed up for a brunch that Rowan insisted Natalie share with them. Demitri's absence was explained as "having run out for something," and her daughter was being treated as if she'd been born into their ranks.

Natalie mumbled something about too much champagne to explain her sullen mood and hid behind the challenge of cutting up enough waffle to keep the boys busy with their blunt plastic forks.

All she wanted was to be gone before Demitri showed up—not that she really expected him to turn up here. If he did, he certainly wouldn't be coming to see her.

The door clicked and all the adult voices dried up, telling her that for all their lighthearted banter, they all knew she and Demitri had blown up last night.

Footsteps came toward her, but she stayed seated at the table, frozen with her back to him, begging lightning to strike her.

"Don't look at me like that," Demitri grumbled to someone. "I'm fixing it."

His hand came into her averted field of vision, gently taking the knife out of her hand, then the fork.

She dropped her head into her hands, covering her eyes. Hiding.

"Come on, Natalie," he said, not angry or aggressive. Firm, but tender. His touch on her shoulder was insistent. "We need to talk."

"Mom?" her daughter questioned, becoming aware of adult attention falling on Natalie and Demitri.

"It's okay, gumdrop. I just need to talk to her for a minute. We'll be right back," Demitri said in that voice that almost sounded… No, she wouldn't tell herself it was loving. "Come on," he urged Natalie. "Or do you want to do it here?"

No.

She rose, vaguely aware of Theo handing Demitri something as they left, only realizing after Demitri had guided her down to the end of the hall that it had been a security card. They entered a private lounge, silent and still, that was probably used for weddings and private dinners. It had a wet bar off to the side and a handful of trendy backless sofas sprinkled throughout. Floor-to-ceiling windows offered a view across Central Park to die for, sunlight glancing off it from a low angle that made it sparkle under the glitter of light snow.

"What I said last night…" she managed in a strained voice, hardly able to face him. "I didn't mean it to sound as though being part of your family isn't good enough for me. Of course they're wonderful. Zoey…" Already meshed. She wished…

"I'd say forget my family, but I don't want you to forget them. They're as much a part of what I'm offering you as I am. They already care about you, Natalie. They're your backup plan, and they're never going to let me get away with hurting you. Not that I'll let myself get away with it," he muttered.

"Because you're afraid of their disapproval? That's

what I meant last night!" She clenched her hands, turning to glance warily at him, holding her breath to try to get through this without busting open.

"I've had nothing but their disapproval all my life. I'm used to it. No," he said firmly. "Their approval is the last thing I was trying to get when I asked you to marry me. I want your love, Natalie."

His words wrung her heart like a wet rag. And scared her, because once her heart was involved, she was a pushover. She shook her head, trying to stop him from continuing, but he approached with purpose. Determination.

"You love me." He was a fallen angel, brutally handsome, sweetly attentive as he committed his cruelty with delicate care, ambling forward so he stood directly in front of her. He tilted up her chin so she couldn't avoid his eyes. "That wasn't part of the fantasy. It's real. Your love is mine, Natalie. And I won't let you show it to me, then refuse to give it to me. I want it. I'm taking it."

She caught back a sob, eyes on fire as she searched for a place to look. Her lips quivered and her throat thickened.

"And I'm going to give you my love so you can show me how to make it better and stronger."

She blinked, trying to see him through her swimming eyes, certain she'd misheard.

His hand cupped her cheek, and he wiped the tears brimming her lashes. "You're going to accept my love, Natalie. You're going to let me give you everything you need. And if I miss something, you're going to tell me so I can do it right."

"It's not that easy. Zoey—"

"You'll help me do right by her, too. And any kids we make together."

"But—"

"No, listen. I realize that your mom put Gareth first. I know she had no choice, but what did that teach you? That your needs come second. Don't throw Zoey at me and tell me she trumps your right to be happy. You don't have to settle for a few weeks of fantasy, Natalie. You can have this all the time. You can have me. You can have a man who pays the bills and sends Zoey to expensive schools and tells you to work for my brother if you want to, not because you have to. I'm going to open my firm in Montreal and stick around, whether you want me there or not, because I want *you*. I want to be with you. I love you."

His words caught and rent deep in her chest, where secret dreams like ice dancing and husbands who came home resided. Where every aspect of her life wasn't all on her. It was a joint venture. A loving, laughing partnership that she'd convinced herself she didn't need.

But she wanted.

So badly.

Was this really happening?

Her brow crinkled as he dug a velvet box out of his pocket and offered her its contents. A diamond ring. "Will you marry me?"

Natalie began to tremble all over, but with a kind of joy that made the world look sprinkled in fairy dust.

"You could have anyone. You know that, right?" she managed to stammer.

"Natalie, you are the only woman I have ever loved. The only one I've ever proposed to. *You* could have anyone, and I will never look lightly on the fact that you are willing to take me. Are you? Will you marry me?"

"Yes," she admitted in a whisper, as though she was confiding it to Santa.

He took the ring and threaded it onto her finger. It was incredibly tasteful, of course. The man could be outrageous, but never tacky or ostentatious.

He kissed her knuckles, then her lips. She clung to the connection, trembling, still not quite believing, but the sweetness of his kiss filled her up so no empty spaces were left.

"I do love you," she told him, awed and humbled by the gratitude and thrill she read in his eyes.

"I love you, too," he said against her lips, pulling her close to crush her with careful arms. Heads tilted together, they both smiled so big they could barely kiss, hearts battering against each other.

"Thank you for coming back," she said sheepishly.

"Always," he promised.

"Should we tell them?" she asked him after they'd shared a few more kisses.

"I want to see Zoey's reaction," he admitted with a rueful grin. "I'm crazy about her, you know. She's as easy to love as her mother."

Their faces must have told the story. The minute they appeared, beaming and glued to each other's side, everyone clapped and champagne bottles were popped. Natalie showed Zoey her ring and said, "Demitri and I are getting married. What do you think of that?"

"I like it," Zoey said, as if she'd been asked to judge the ring. "It's pretty. If you get married, does that mean you can have a baby? 'Cause I want a little brother."

EPILOGUE

NATALIE EMERGED TO typical chaos in the back garden of Rosedale, Nic and Rowan's Greek island home. The men were barbecuing and talking politics around watching the children. The women were back and forth to the kitchen, trying to keep everyone sunscreened, fed and hydrated.

Oh, how Natalie loved when they were all together like this. It wasn't easy, but they made the children's birthdays a priority and Evie's was tomorrow.

"Who did you find?" Demitri asked Natalie, coming forward to take their nearly three-year-old nephew, Zephyr, off her hip. He'd been cuddly while he'd still been sleepy, but now he energized as he leaped for his uncle. Demitri gave him a light toss in the air before kissing his grinning cheek. "About time you woke up, champ. Everyone's been asking for you. Zoey," he called across to where the children were taking turns riding down the minislide into the little wading pool. "Look who woke up."

"Jaya's awake, too," Natalie said in answer to Theo's questioning glance. "She'll be out in a minute." They'd all converged here this morning, but jet lag was taking its toll on some more than others.

Demitri handed off Zephyr to Zoey and came to hook his arm around Natalie's waist, always affectionate, but especially so when he was relaxed and happy, as he was when they were around his family.

"Zoey, you don't have to carry him," Jaya said as she

came outside and gravitated to her husband. She still sounded sleepy, and Theo cuddled her into his side, rubbing her back.

"I like to," Zoey said, turning back with Zephyr clinging to her like a rhesus monkey. He was half her seven-year-old height and she was all bones these days, growing like a cornstalk, front teeth missing so she lisped. "I carry my other cousins all the time." She started to turn away, then turned back again. "Mom, you said I'd probably never have cousins from you, only from Daddy. Now I have four."

"I know. We did pretty good, eh?" Natalie said.

"We did," Zoey said with a nod of approval, and bore her cousin away.

"Eh?" Rowan repeated in a light tease. "I used to think that was a joke, but you Canadians really say it. Even Demitri's started."

"How many cousins does she have on the other side?" Nic asked.

"It's not a competition," Natalie chided, sharing an eye-roll with the other wives. Theo was mature enough to abstain from juvenile contests, but the other three were not.

"I'm just saying, if we could assist in any way…" Nic continued innocently.

Rowan tilted her head back in a sultry laugh of enjoyment, hugging her husband. "We've been dying to get you all together and tell you! The agency called us. They have a little boy from the same village as Evie. We can get him next week, and we were hoping one of you would keep Evie while we do."

"Of course," everyone rushed to agree, hugging and kissing and congratulating.

As the hullaballoo died down, Adara said, "Of course, that's only one." She shared a look with her husband, flashed one at Jaya and bit her lip. "We have a bit of news ourselves. You know that we've never wanted to open the can of worms that is Gideon's background, so adoption has never really been available to us. But a friend of Jaya's cousin is pregnant. She's very young, but wants to have the baby and have an open-adoption situation. We've talked with her several times and… Of course, anything could happen, but she seems very certain."

"We offered to help her out so she can keep it, but she wants to finish her education and go into law. She's met Androu," Gideon said, indicating their son. "She feels strongly that we can offer a better upbringing. They both do. The baby's father is in the picture, willing to marry her, but he really doesn't have much. And he's scared out of his mind at the idea of being a father. Doesn't feel he'd make a good parent. He'd rather his child have more stability and opportunity."

"She's due in a month and… Well, as I say, things can change, but I think we're expecting," Adara said with a teary smile.

All the women sighed and hugged her; the men kissed her cheek and shook Gideon's hand. Everyone wished them luck.

"So that's two," Demitri said with a nod of approval. "Of course, my brother the math whiz might say differently. How is your wife's jet lag slash food poisoning, anyway?"

"Okay, it's not food poisoning!" Jaya cried, covering the blush that darkened her cheeks. "And it must be a girl because I was never this sick with Zephyr." As she accepted congratulations from everyone, she said, "I hated keeping it from all of you. It's just that silly rule about—"

"Waiting three months, I know," Demitri said. "Bothers me, too."

Everyone went quiet. They looked at his smirk, transferred their attention to Natalie's flushing cheeks and exasperated glance at her husband. They grinned.

Adara blinked back tears and said, "Oh, Natalie."

"I know," Natalie said, growing teary herself. It wasn't just hormones. She was happy. Really, really happy. They'd been waiting until his business was established, which had happened very quickly, given his skill and connections. She was finishing up a special project she and Jaya had been working on for the hotels and now…

Life was about as perfect as it got.

After accepting everyone's felicitations, she hugged Demitri, reveling in the way he gently crushed her into his side.

"Thank you," she whispered. "For giving me all of this."

"Thank *you*," he said, grazing her lips with his own. "I never imagined myself like this, you know."

"A father? Part of a big family?"

"Happy," he corrected. "Living happily-ever-after."

* * * * *

MILLS & BOON®

MODERN™

POWER, PASSION AND IRRESISTIBLE TEMPTATION

A sneak peek at next month's titles...

In stores from 19th June 2015:

- **The Ruthless Greek's Return** – Sharon Kendrick
- **Married for Amari's Heir** – Maisey Yates
- **Sicilian's Shock Proposal** – Carol Marinelli
- **The Sheikh's Wedding Contract** – Andie Brock

In stores from 3rd July 2015:

- **Bound by the Billionaire's Baby** – Cathy Williams
- **A Taste of Sin** – Maggie Cox
- **Vows Made in Secret** – Louise Fuller
- **One Night, Two Consequences** – Joss Wood

Available at WHSmith, Tesco, Asda, Eason, Amazon and Apple

Just can't wait?
Buy our books online a month before they hit the shops!
visit www.millsandboon.co.uk

These books are also available in eBook format!